D0487657

The Other Side

The novels of Stanley Middleton

The Other Side

STANLEY MIDDLETON

Hutchinson & Co. (Publishers) Ltd
An imprint of the Hutchinson Publishing Group

Hutchinson Group (Australia) Pty Ltd
30–32 Cremorne Street, Richmond South, Victoria 3121
PO Box 151, Broadway, New South Wales 2007

Hutchinson Group (NZ) Ltd
32–34 View Road, PO Box 40-086, Glenfield, Auckland 10

Hutchinson Group (SA) (Pty) Ltd
PO Box 337, Bergvlei 2012, South Africa

First published 1980

© Stanley Middleton 1980

Set in Intertype Plantin 11pt

Printed in Great Britain by
The Anchor Press Ltd and bound by
Wm Brendon & Son Ltd
both of Tiptree, Essex

British Library Cataloguing in Publication Data

Middleton, Stanley
The other side.
I. Title
823'.9'1F   PR6063.I250/

ISBN 0 09 143750 4

Hutchinson
London Melbourne Sydney Auckland Johannesburg

Hutchinson & Co. (Publishers) Ltd
An imprint of the Hutchinson Publishing Group
3 Fitzroy Square, London WIP 6JD

Hutchinson Group (Australia) Pty Ltd
30–32 Cremorne Street, Richmond South, Victoria 3121
PO Box 151, Broadway, New South Wales 2007

Hutchinson Group (NZ) Ltd
32–34 View Road, PO Box 40–086, Glenfield, Auckland 10

Hutchinson Group (SA) (Pty) Ltd
PO Box 337, Bergvlei 2012, South Africa

First published 1980

© Stanley Middleton 1980

Set in Intertype Plantin 11pt

Printed in Great Britain by
The Anchor Press Ltd and bound by
Wm Brendon & Son Ltd
both of Tiptree, Essex

British Library Cataloguing in Publication Data

Middleton, Stanley
    The other side.
    I. Title
    823'.9'1F   PR6063.1250/

ISBN 0 09 143750 4

To Harold Harris,
with thanks

He passed by on the other side.
St Luke

So he passed over, and all the trumpets
He passed by on the other side.
Bunyan

I

In sunshine the Easter Monday queue for the Castle length-
ened under black stone of the medieval gate. Never more than
a straggling three wide, it took a right-angled twist towards
the turnstile where the officials seemed, as usual, in no sort
of hurry. White cloud against blue sky was reflected below
in the bright frocks and shirts under the smoke-dark tunnel
with its inbuilt room, marked by a poster: Civic Society
Shop. The rising lawns spread trimly; railings had been
freshly painted; smartness shone the order of the day.

Just as the woman and her child emerged, were about to
turn right, a young attendant in uniform hopped the low,
grass-green palings, fumbled at a lock, opened a gate.

'This way, please. Save you queueing.'

The small girl pulled at her mother's arm, but she had
hesitated and half a dozen had pressed in front.

'Steady, Miranda,' she warned.

The attendant, pale-eyed with long fair hair, smiled for
the first time as the youngster handed over their 10p
piece.

'Two, is it?' He tore off the tickets from a roll lying on
the ground behind him. 'Don't forget them.'

They were through, and the child pulled hard, burst from
her mother's grasp, and running forward a yard or two,
turned back.

'We didn't go through that turnstile.'

'Whose fault's that?'

Cloud obscured the sun, and suddenly it blew cold. Elizabeth Watson, glad she'd decided on a coat, pulled the collar
together. Miranda was chugging uphill, winding in and out

of the groups ahead of her mother, who did not call out, or even watch her closely. Some people squatted on the grass, as if in the warmth of high summer. Away to the right a small girl roly-polied down a steep bank, almost dangerously, but stopped halfway, and picking herself up, found the slope nearly too great for safe standing.

A red-cheeked man, coming towards Mrs Watson said, face creased, 'We must all be mad,' and passed on. She smelt beer.

The flower beds had been weeded, and primula, streaked tulip, crocus, scilla and chionodoxa, she wasn't certain, brightened at the eye-wiping, sudden return of the sun. Order existed here except for the people who walked purposefully if they took the path, but lost all force, or idea of direction, once they wandered on to the turf. Uniformed nurses wheeled two old men in chairs down the sharp gradient, laughing at their speed. Both patients, wrapped in tartan blankets, were grey-faced, the first with his eyes shut tight, the second his mouth agape with apprehension; knuckles white claw-hooks.

'Don't you let 'em go,' a middle-aged man shouted jovially. The nurses laughed again, and slapped the handles of their chairs to demonstrate control.

'Which way?'

Miranda waited for her mother at the bottom of the broad stone steps, which were, surprisingly, empty.

'Straight up.'

The child dashed off, and as Elizabeth toiled after her she noticed that now people followed her, did not take the easier slope to the right. No one knew his mind, her wish. Miranda danced at the top, and when her mother joined her grabbed her hand, continuing to skip. Strollers smiled at them.

'My, I wish I'd that amount of energy.' A man on a seat, walking-stick neatly alongside stretched legs, grey hair combed back from his forehead spoke, delighted at a twenty-nine

8

year old, beautiful woman and her lively child. He unpinned an artificial rose from his lapel, handed it to the daughter. 'Say thank you.'

The child complied, both shy and forward, twirling the little bloom.

Elizabeth Watson moved on, a smile drying from her lips, legs weary already. She disliked artificial flowers, on good days, could see no sense in them however well made, real-seeming. Again Miranda broke away, bounding forward. The mother, who was tall, slim, with stylish clothes, upswept hair, walked with steady steps, beautifully elegant, looking neither to right nor left, the slight pallor and severity of her face adding to her attraction. Heads turned when she passed.

Now Miranda had reached the low wall above the castle rock, and stood craning on the railings behind the thin stone-work. Beyond, square miles of factories, sidings, a length of canal scarred the land, slightly blurred even on this fine afternoon, and under the wall, she knew, toppled the rock, the sandstone cliff, the unseen drop to the road with its coloured cars between buildings, brick, glass, terraced messu-ages, factories, old-fashioned offices, warehouses. Elizabeth's belly contracted as the child leaned forward, dress ends flapping, but she refused to shout a warning, stood with her daughter, felt almost grateful when the child groped for her hand.

'Could anybody climb down there?' A boy asked, too loudly.

'Mountaineers,' an older brother answered.

'Don't you get trying it.' His father, lighting one cigarette from another in the wind.

'You could get killed.' The boy sounded eager.

Elizabeth stared over the flat land, a river valley, darkly industrial but antiquated, as if steam and coal furnaces thrashed the machines, coating the world with soot, blacken-ing stunted grass. New factories electrically powered, four-square and colourless, stood further off, only vaguely tarnished by the oil streaks, the murk, the heavy clank of energy inefficiently applied. Even today, Easter holiday, smudges of smoke pothered, were whipped haphazard, chased and shredded against the clean sky.

'I wouldn't like to fall down there,' Miranda said.

'Be careful, then.'

'Has anybody?'

'Yes, I think they have.'

'My great-grand-dad did.' One of the boys, eyes aggressive, lower lip forward, provoked perhaps by her accent. 'He committed suicide.'

'Nobody wants to hear that.' The father, smiling apologetically, glasses askew, rebuked him. The man, she noted with distaste, did not remove his cigarette to speak. His lips were yellow. Suddenly he waved his charges on.

'Well, he did. You said so yourself.' His son was outraged at his father's treason.

'Are you warm enough?' Elizabeth asked. Her child stood upright, shoes wedged between the railings, waving her arms, as if preparing to fly. There was no danger, but even in her misery the mother disliked the oddness of the whirling movement, the implied defiance of gravity.

'Did you come here when you were a little girl?' The seven-year-old had descended, was dragging her mother on. She knew the answer well enough, but it might be that some other information would appear; one could not always decide with adults.

'No, I didn't live here. I was grown up before I came. We went to Windsor Castle.'

'Is that better than this?'

'I should think so.'

Children clambered at the telescope, to spend five pence bringing fields or a tree nearer, eliminating the factories. Miranda walked past, a stately seven-year-old, unwilling to line up even if she wanted a turn, or fearful of refusal. Ahead now they could see in the distance the university, its pink hospital, all as static as the workshops, cardboard palaces and towers in spring brightness. Nearer to the right were the mansions where Victorian lace manufacters had lived, in arboreal comfort, behind stained-glass doors big enough for churches and in gardens wide enough for cricket. From this height the grand houses looked pinched, the roads mean, and the trees' black outlines wintry still.

They turned to the entrance of the building at the end of a flat crescent of pillars, interspersed with busts of literary persons.

'Look at his nose, mam; i'n't it big?' A strapping lad pointed at Henry Kirke White, read out his name.

The door, crowded and narrow, people coming and going, queuing, into comparative darkness.

'Do you want to go down Mortimer's Hole?' Elizabeth forced herself to ask. Miranda shuddered, shaking her head.

'The cat,' she said, leading the way. Her mother followed meekly, confused, uncertainly pleased that the child knew her mind. She found herself sighing; the sound surprised her, but nobody paid attention.

The room dedicated to Egyptian antiquities had little to recommend it, but Miranda was already kneeling at a handsome show cabinet, smiling up at her mother, wanting her to share the moment. Her finger pointed in anticipation at a brown bundle of varnished bandages, dried stiff, unrecognizable, a mummified parcel, the cat. She registered intense pleasure, perhaps at finding the object.

'It is fascinating to think that this creature lived and died before Jesus Christ.' Elizabeth turned to look at the speaker, expecting a grey-haired, paunchy, impressive man from the authoritarian tone. All the world instructed today if one listened. A small, neatly bearded fellow, perhaps thirty odd, enlightened his bespectacled wife, and three extraordinarily clean children, nodding his head. His wife's eyes sparkled; she expected instruction, appreciated its advent. Even the children listened. Miranda withdrew her attention from the case to the family, slightly frowning, as if this statement had impudently encapsulated the mystery of attraction and thus had killed it. Elizabeth said nothing.

'I like that,' Miranda challenged. Her mother did not answer. 'Daddy says he couldn't tell it was a cat. I could. Or an animal, anyway. Did they have rabbits?'

'I don't know.'

The family had passed on. Little Mr Know-All might have come up with the information, the Egyptian word, the hieroglyph for vermin. Didn't the Bible talk about coneys? Were they . . . ? Elizabeth's mind lurched past the questions, into misery again.

'I would like a word with you, Elizabeth.'

Thus David her husband had begun three evenings ago, on Good Friday as they stood washing up after the evening meal. Could she claim now she had been expecting such a formal summons? She did not know. Certainly he did not usually speak so solemnly.

'All right. Go on, then.' Lightly.

'When we have finished.'

They completed the task in silence together, though they could hear Miranda chattering to her grandfather from the sitting-room. She did not hurry, biting her lips, dismissing premonition, determined to be awkward, although she had not an idea what he was about to announce. In spite of the day he'd been at work and had not changed from his office clothes this evening. Usually as soon as he came in the door, and shouted his greeting, he'd run upstairs to put on his denim trousers, his T-shirt. Today he rolled down his shirt sleeves, refastened his cufflinks, put on his jacket. The smart executive gently pulled at his waistcoat, buttoned his coat, moved his right hand over his already smooth, thick hair.

'Somewhere out of the way,' he said, almost in undertone. 'Where it's quiet.'

'Bedroom?'

'That'll do.'

She poked her head into the sitting-room to warn Miranda and grandpa that they'd need to occupy themselves a short while longer. They raised no objection.

The bedroom, which faced south, dazzled with light still at seven o'clock. David stood, princely fashion, with hands behind his back against the long wardrobe mirror; she passed him saying nothing, occupied a chair against the window, folding her hands in her lap. She felt fright as her breath came in short gulps, but she forced herself to look at his face. He did not return the glance, stared at the grey reproduction of steamers at Trent Bridge over the bed. He appeared more puzzled than concerned, as if he needed her advice. Her legs trembled.

She waited; she would make him start.

'I don't know how to say this, Liz.'

That needn't be answered. She froze.

'We haven't been getting on too well, recently.' She watched. 'Well, have we?' Anger flashed in his voice, but she stared on. He looked at her only briefly, as he rolled his head, like a man at physiotherapy. 'The fault's mine, I'm willing to admit. Or the major part.'

In this elegant bedroom, his voice suggested depth, rather than sounded deeply, while his slight northern accent, he came from Sheffield, added an ultra-ingredient, he thought and spoke like an advertisement, sincerity. She wished to God he'd shift his hands from behind his stiff back, posing there.

'Even so, what I am going to say now will come as a shock to you.'

Her mind scrambled furiously for meaning. Had he given up his job? That seemed unlikely, and had no connection with their broken relations, and yet it came first into her head. The management man. Now he bit his lower lip, nodded his head deliberately, hunching his shoulders. She found extreme difficulty in breathing.

'I'm going to leave you.'

The pang which rammed her breast had little to do with understanding; the gravity of his tone was enough. If he had said, 'I'm going to buy you a new car' in that voice her heart would have faltered, struggled, before blessed relief flooded. She did not budge.

'I'm going to live with Gill Paige.'

She knew the name, had met the woman, but the sentence made not much sense. A flare of late, low sunshine lit one side of the huge bow window, flashing, then quite gradually disappeared, like an ill-timed stage effect. He was blowing out his lips, waiting for the comment she was determined not to give. He turned on his heel away from her.

'That's it, then.' Twelve feet, thirteen perhaps, separated them. He took two big steps doorwards, then stopped, back broad, fingers intertwisted. As she looked over the grey suit, the large white hands, she felt she felt nothing, except that by keeping her mouth shut, she'd frighten him more. He was despicable.

'Haven't you anything to say, then?' He bullied. She would not reward him with a word, looked out of the window, down the large front gardens, the gravelled drives, the status-symbol cars, the lime trees. She heard him slap his pockets; he'd shifted his hands then. 'I'm sorry,' he said. 'I'm truly sorry.'

She knew that if she spoke she'd cry. He waited.

'Oh, well, then.' He whispered petulantly, left her. She heard the footsteps on the thick of the stair carpet, the faint creak of a well-made banister violently pushed. Her mind set hard, disappeared from her so that she was left staring down the garden without impression now, without knowledge of herself or the external world, only an insistence from inside that she sit. How long she remained so she had little idea, but when she stood her legs trembled so that she stumbled towards the dressing table. Leaning, she glared into the mirror, lunged for the door, and feeling her way along the wall went into the lavatory. She tiptoed, giddy as she swayed, and bolted the door silently, determined not to betray herself with noise.

As soon as she sat a sob crouped upwards, her resistance shattered and she wept. Stifling the sound with a square inch or two of handkerchief she rolled in an agony of shock, mindlessly, taken over by the mechanics of grief. It seemed that the paroxysm would not end, that she'd be found at midnight, in the small hours, at dawn crouched there, eyes running, mouth distorting, shoulders and lungs heaving. She abandoned the scrap of linen and lace for soft toilet paper, dabbed, screwed, dropped the darkened crumples.

She discovered that she had become silent. The pain in her chest and back gnawed as desperately, but it was static. Her face felt lacerated, bruised, blubbered beyond recognition or repair. She tried her feet, found she could stand. She used the lavatory, gathered the paper from the floor, dropped it into the pan, and then when she had flushed the cistern listened for some return signal from downstairs. In the bathroom she washed herself, surprised that the crying jag had left so little trace. Back in the bedroom she changed her blouse, spent, overspent time on her hair, made her face up discreetly. Ten minutes to eight.

Before she went down she returned to the lavatory to check she had left it tidy. She had. She walked very slowly downstairs, into the sitting-room, dreading the sound of her own voice.

Her husband sat at the table, briefcase open, a neat scatter of typewritten sheets before him. He wore his glasses, black-sided. His father occupied an armchair by the hearth, a newspaper spread on his knee, passing time uncomfortably, not even feigning interest in his grand-daughter who, on the rug at his feet, tapped at a dulcimer.

'Listen, mummy.'

The child, fastidiously, in a slow accurate rhythm, pinged out, 'Twinkle, twinkle, little star; how I wonder what you are.'

'Very good.' Nothing wrong with her voice. 'It's bedtime now.'

'But, mummy, it's not eight o'clock.'

'By the time you've had a drink and cleaned your teeth . . .'

'It will be past it.'

Elizabeth could not laugh at the prissy imitation, but the child picked up her dulcimer obediently, stood ready.

'Say goodnight, then.'

Miranda held her face up to her grandfather. The old man smiled, but looked suspiciously at the mother. Perhaps he would have liked to throw his arms round the girl. He rattled his paper, pushing the glasses up his nose, kissed the child.

'Goodnight, daddy.'

David gestured with his spectacles off, bent to his daughter.

'Be good,' he called, as the two left the room.

'Come and see me when I'm in bed.'

'I will.'

Elizabeth tucked the girl away, and then fitted herself up in the spare room. She collected what she would need, morning and evening, and that night spent sleepless hours in the strange place. David did not call in, but she trusted his father to ask inquisitive questions.

had cleaned and washed the breakfast things, her husband confessed. Elizabeth said, 'Are we going to the Hilton, then?' She shrugged but did not attempt to move away. He looked pale; well, unshaven, jumpy; he had not changed his shirt.
'Mira—'

2

Miranda occupied herself at length at the showcase.

Her mother, uncertain of herself, stood out of the way neither watching the child nor bothering herself with the constantly changing, chattering figures who shuffled vaguely out in front. Suddenly looking up, she saw Miranda, white-faced, straining towards her.

'What's wrong?' The girl hugged her arm.

'I'd lost you. I thought you'd gone out to see the pictures.'

'When?'

'A long time. You weren't there.'

'I haven't moved from this spot.'

Now the child recovered, smiled, did a dancing step, but clung still to her mother.

'I went as far as "Blind Homer".'

'You don't like that.'

'I know. And it wasn't very light there.'

'And where was I supposed to be, miss?'

'I don't know.'

'You must have gone wandering off on your own. Again.'

'Yes.' A serious pause. 'I frightened myself.'

Elizabeth, herself scared at the lost time, stepped out, relieved, jolted if minutely from the flat ache of misery. On Saturday last she had prepared breakfast, but had pointedly refused conversation with her husband. She would pass toast, butter, marmalade, but to questions requiring verbal answers she sat stone deaf. David soon desisted, but not before Miranda and grandfather had noticed, gaped.

They had arranged to go out for lunch at the Hilton, a new departure, in that old Mr Watson confessed the awkwardness he felt in such surroundings, but he had been persuaded three days before and David had booked a table. When the men had cleared and washed the breakfast things, her husband cornered Elizabeth, said, 'Are we going to the Hilton, then?'

She shrugged but did not attempt to move away. He looked not well, unshaven, jumpy; he had not changed his shirt.

'Make your mind up,' he rasped.

This time she spread her hands, continental fashion, ironically.

'It's to give you a break,' he said, not quite shouting, face flushed. That was weak.

'All right.' And she shoved past him, dreading a blow, a clutch at the cloth of her shoulder, a staggering push, but he did not touch her. She almost wished for a martyrdom in violence.

She made the meal uncomfortable, kept them waiting, refused point blank to make any social conversation with her husband. David, flustered as his father, tried to pass it off by joking with Miranda, drawing her attention to waiters or wine glasses, but the girl, in the middle of one of his best flights, which had raised a smile from the old man, suddenly turned away and put a sympathetic hand on the crook of her mother's arm. That dried his wit.

Afterwards they went down to the river, watched the swans on the wind-eddied surface, shivered. David grabbed Miranda's hand and the pair skipped away among the daffodils, the man singing brashly.

'Are you . . . ? Is anything . . . ?' Watson did his best.

'Don't you worry,' she said.

'Ah, but I do.'

Tears blasted her eyes. She could blame the east wind as they stumped along, for she determined not to give any explanation to her father-in-law. David was still afraid, though he'd not admit, of the old chap. John Barrett Watson, retired engine driver, had lived life quietly for the last ten years as a widower, and had only joined them since Christmas. His son mocked the Primitive Methodism under which he had grown up, but it offered certainties which he lacked now, and, to be fair, did not want. Expediency, a quick turn-over, the dishing of a rival firm, a sound investment, a house in the right district depended on the sharp eye, not the cast-iron commandment. The father did not say much; he did not need, since he had brought his boy up to know what was right, but he looked round the present large house, their third change, bought last summer, appreciatively, guessing every penny of its value, hands deep in his pocket and a text written in the wrinkles of his forehead: Thou fool, this night thy soul shall be required of thee.

'I'll say this,' Watson spoke now, breathily, phlegm rattling, 'David's fond of that child.'

'Yes.' She watched the two cavort.

'Will you be having any more? We couldn't, somehow. Annie had a rough time with him. We should have liked a girl. After Jennifer.'

'We'll see.' She felt sorry; the man's face paled blue-white. It wasn't much more than a year ago since the heart attack that had reduced him finally to their house. Even so, he had not sold off his semi in Sheffield, but let it furnished, believing he'd return. 'You look frozen. Let's go back to the car.'

'Best give 'em a shout.'

'They'll see.'

They turned; she would have taken his arm, if she had not believed, wrongly, that he'd have shaken her off. The wind stung. Watson put his head down; the pace was funeral. When they reached the car, the others had not caught them up, were not in sight.

'Let's go over to that seat. It'll be out of the wind.' She'd no keys for David's Rover. 'They shouldn't be long.'

They sat together until she was almost petrified. Miranda windmilled up, cheeks reddened, hair blown wild.

'Where's Daddy?' The child pointed vaguely behind.

'He's looking for you.'

'Go and tell him to hurry up. Granddad's frozen.'

The child looked dashed. She did not fancy a return trip to an angry father. Usually her mother would have gone, and she be ordered to stay here, not move a muscle until all was sorted out.

'I don't know where he is.'

'Sit down, then.' Miranda never disobeyed that voice. Elizabeth stood, looked about for her husband who could not be seen, even in the thinning numbers. People walked hard, swung their arms, turned collars up. No other idiots patronized the benches. She was still standing when David appeared, brow black as thunder.

'Where the hell . . . ?' he began.

His wife pointed across her chest at his father. Watson's eyes were closed; his lips blue. They had him inside the car with the engine running in no time, so that he soon recovered, refused fuss. On the comfortable back seat, Miranda leaned in comfort on her mother, singing casually to herself, in her own world.

Immediately after an awkward tea, David disappeared, presumably to spend the evening with Gill Paige. Liz did not hear his return. On Sunday he drove off just before 7 p.m., and this morning had announced at breakfast that he had work to do, away from home.

'It's the bank holiday,' his father had objected.

'This is a social engagement, which will have results, we hope.'

'You've a family.'

'I know, but every job has its drawbacks. When you were on a night shift, I didn't see you and had to creep about like a ghost all day.'

'Ghosts don't creep,' Miranda said.

'They don't make noise. They glide,' David answered, 'very silently.'

'They howl, sometimes.'

'Isn't that a banshee?'

'I gave my wife notice,' Watson said. He scrubbed the back of his head roughly with a knuckle.

'You were lucky.'

They said no more, but damage had been done. When David left, he pushed a card into his wife's hand. 'I'm having lunch with Sir William Whittaker. That's his phone number in case I'm needed. Any time after one-thirty.' It was now half past nine. She dropped the rectangle on to the nearest table, and turned away unspeaking. Her husband groaned, but she was already out of the room.

After lunch, Mr Watson said he wouldn't accompany them to the castle, but settle for a nap. He shook his head widely.

'I don't know what he's up to.'

'I've told you not to worry.'

'With him it's business before everything.'

'Did you ever have to work on Sundays?' she asked.

'Ay. Yes. Not often. And I didn't like doing it. Six days shalt thou labour, and on the seventh do the odd jobs.' He smiled; that was meant to cheer her up. He'd pose riddles next. 'There comes a time when you've got to put wife and family first. If you don't, it means trouble before too long.'

Miranda this Monday afternoon skipped, as if the movement of sightseers excited her.

'What next?' Elizabeth asked.

' "Blind Homer." '

'You don't like it.'

'Well, I do really.'

They walked the long gallery where people stumbled, craning upward or peering down, at landscapes, fine faces, nacreous ladies. Children crammed into booths for their peep show, calling out in surprise or for information. The painting they sought, a large French oil, 'Blind Homer Singing at the Gates of Troy', attracted little attention in its position of honour in the middle of a smaller room as the two came through the door. On the walls were a few exquisite Bonington watercolours, and one or two of his oils, dull as the others were luminous.

Miranda adopted her usual pose, head on one side.

'I don't like his face,' she said.

'He looks blind.'

'What is he singing about?'

'Presumably the war between the Greeks and the Trojans. But I don't know whether he did that. At Troy, I mean. I think he was born in Asia Minor.'

The child, satisfied, for she had elicited this answer before, walked off. Elizabeth, murmuring a warning, chased after her daughter, wondering why once again she'd forgotten to consult the encyclopedia and the classical dictionary. In six months' time they'd be back with the same question still unanswered, the identical twinge of guilt.

They found their way outside where sunshine and chill winds kept people on the move. Rounding the castle, they walked the paths, past the statue of Capt. Albert Ball, vc, who crumbled slightly under the protective angel behind him, past the deserted bandstand. These paths at whatever time of year were darted across by shouting, unaccompanied children, intent on mobile quarrels. Miranda at first refused, then bought an iced lolly; she tongued it modestly, knowing she had somehow failed to pass an examination in taste, resenting her weakness while enjoying its synthetic fruits. They stared down the walls on to the statue of Robin Hood, whose bow vandals had left arrowless.

'Will yo' come back 'ere?' A ferocious blast of anger from a short woman waddling behind a pushchair. A boy, five perhaps, but undersized, dodged behind a tree, hair tufty. 'Do yo' 'ear w'arr I say?'

He did and edged an inch or two nearer the tree. Miranda, legs apart, had taken up a position of vantage. 'Will yo' bring that bleddy bag back an' gi'e it to our Samantha?' The voice

22

bawled with egregious power. The lad peered out, unabashed, as his mother continued her fleshy advance. 'When I get there, I'll 'afe kill you. Now gi'e it 'er back.' The boy slid out, approached his mother and her chair, which was flanked by a crying girl, a year older than the wrongdoer, and a smaller male version. As the boy sidled up, his mother remarkably quickened her pace, but he dodged and thrust the offending paper bag into the hands of the younger brother, who, hardly interested, handed it across to the sister. Like a fury the woman snatched the bag, abandoned the pushchair, which toppled, as she dashed the booty into the chest of the felon who now, with an expression not unlike Miranda's, stood to watch developments.

'Gi'e it our Sam when you're to'd.'

He handed it over.

'Fawce bogger.' Only now did she right the pushchair, the occupant of which had made not a whimper. 'And don't yo' be so bleddy daft as to lerr' him gerr o'd on it again.'

The woman began to waddle forward, her party in line, when she glanced up and noticed Miranda, who held ground. For a moment Elizabeth expected another blast of invective, but the pig-small eyes took in the well-dressed mother behind the observing child, and nothing was attempted, except the cracked, buckled shoes were scraped more noisily along the tarmacadam. The family paid no attention, grasping the uprights, rustling the bag, pressing on God knows where.

'That boy was disobedient,' Miranda spoke, skipped away from further comment.

The two completed their round, exchanging usual questions and answers on the fifteenth century house re-erected outside across the road, and made their way back through the gate, where the queue stretched longer. As they negotiated the turnstile the young man appeared once more to allow people through his small fence, chivvying. They walked the streets, patted Robin Hood's bronze flanks, admired elegant houses preserved from the city's planners, walked past warehouses, closed restaurants and shops.

'Daddy's office,' Miranda announced. 'Waterhouse, Cliff Ltd, Engineering Products', the lower right of six similar plaques.

'He doesn't work here,' Elizabeth answered. 'I didn't know they had a place . . . .'

'Who works here, then?'

'You'll have to ask him.'

She would, and David would explain, solemnly in adult language, making no concession to childishness, the ins and outs of the business transacted here. Elizabeth had taken great pleasure in these exchanges which reflected so well on both parties.

They caught the bus, which had trapped the warmth of the sun. The child loved riding on public transport, and showed it by her extraordinary stillness, as if by wriggling she'd miss the visual and auditory treats. Sometimes she'd touch her mother's arm to point out some passing miracle, but Elizabeth had now more sense than to ask what she was supposed to look at. She'd probably learn from a question when the journey was over.

'What was that man doing to his tree?' or 'I wonder why they were carrying those buckets.'

Once they were off the bus, Miranda would skip, and call, and run, expending all her energy in motion.

Grandfather had prepared the tea, had cut his most delicate slices, and laid the table with fine china.

'What's the best thing you saw?' he asked Miranda. She answered immediately. 'What,' he mocked, 'you went all that way just to see a dead cat?'

'That cat was alive before Jesus Christ,' the child said.

The old man beamed; he loved pert answers, thought them over.

'You're a sharp blade,' he said.

24

'She heard some man say that in the museum,' Elizabeth deflated.

'And he was right.' Miranda, like her father putting them all in place.

Soon after seven-thirty David returned, said he wanted nothing to eat, offered to see Miranda to bed.

'Old Possum tonight,' he promised. But he seemed displeased.

'Who's Old Possum?' Watson asked, when the pair had gone. Elizabeth explained, recited a verse of Macavity. The old man shook his head at the notion that so much intellectual pleasure available to the human race had passed him by.

David took to his study without returning downstairs.

'What is he playing at?' Watson worried.

'He's perhaps picked up an idea or two, and wants to work on them.'

'He could have come down and said so, couldn't he?' the father-in-law sniffed. 'There's no need for him to act like a child. He was never so when he was younger, was he now? I mean, he's thirty-eight, not eight.' Watson did not need answers, advanced his views in a grumbling tenor.

Elizabeth remembered her first meeting with her husband.

At the end of her initial term at university, she'd gone to the Engineers' Ball, a notable occasion, full dress, a group and a band. She was sitting with her girl friend, who like her wondered what sort of return they'd get on the rather expensive tickets, when a young man asked her to dance. He was the second of the evening, broad shouldered, stretching his coat, and with a medallion on a thin, silk ribbon round his neck. To her he seemed rather old, so that she wondered if he were a member of staff. The duty group performed with such violence that they had no chance to talk, but he smiled at her, in a satisfied way, and accompanied her back to her seat, saying that he had to attend to something, but he hoped they could dance together later.

Elizabeth's friend, Jo Turle, showed excitement.

'I didn't know you knew him,' she said.

'I don't.'

'You don't know his name?'

'Should I?'

'That's Dave Watson, President of the Engineering Students.' It explained the ribbon. The engineers were a law to themselves, rather older than students in other faculties, with experience in industry, with careers already mapped. They dressed more neatly, disregarded the furious political arguments, scorned egalitarianism, seemed already middle-aged. They occupied no administrative blocks, sat-in no-where, did not openly discuss these matters. Schoolboys could play at being men if they wished; Eng. Soc. got on with it. Their social events were rare, but much talked about; when they broke out it was traditionally with beer and moderate horseplay. Until this evening Elizabeth had not spoken to one of their number, and had only attended the dance at the importunity of her senior, Jo, now a third year. The breathless excitement of this announcement communicated itself to Elizabeth. Her debut had been noticed, and from then on she did not lack partners.

At the interval David came across and insisted that she and Joanna ate at the buffet table he patronized, and where two professors and their wives exchanged sociable words with them. They treated David with some deference, she thought, speaking as to a respected equal. Their topics held no interest for her, but she realized that it was enough to stand still, smile, and be beautiful. In time, the wife of the professor of civil engineering asked her if she were a student, and what she was reading.

'English.'

'Oh, yes. We live next door to Professor Dalgliesh.'

This was high life. The day after next she'd catch the train for London and the Christmas vacation, but now she

26

made her mark. She had whispered to David her name, her hostel; he gave the impression that he was not going home for more than two days, though whether he stayed for a conference, a project, or union business she did not learn. He impressed her without trying. The second half of the proceedings opened with ballroom dancing and the head of the engineering department, a knight no less, was instructed by David to take Elizabeth to inaugurate the traditional snowball quickstep. When, quite at random, she chose her second partner, the boy was terrified and treated her like the Queen.

She remembered those days still hardly believing what she recalled.

David had written a couple of letters, rather short but encouraging, informing her that he was hard at work into the small hours. Her studies had never occupied her to those lengths. She replied in scrawl, describing their Christmas frolics, her cooking or shopping, the Anglo-Saxon she struggled with, and amused him, or so his second letter asserted. On her first day back to university he rang her hall, arranging to see her on the Saturday following. They attended a college hop, drove out for an hour to a local hostelry in a friend's car, shivered by the cloud-darkened lake in scuds of rain, warm within themselves. He outlined his programme of study and leisure for the term, not boastfully, but frightening her by his grasp of essentials. He commanded his time.

Thus they spent one evening a week only, on Saturday, together, though they'd lunch on Wednesday and Thursday in refectory and occasionally meet by chance for coffee, but this was enough to make Elizabeth a person of consequence. Before, she had been a fresher, good looking enough to fill up her evenings at the dances or to be invited here and there, but now, as David Watson's girl, the warden would stop her for a word, and she was elected to hall committee, to the magazine staff, to the secretaryship of the English Society,

27

whence she wrote and spoke to poets, herself decorating the platform.

The university was never the same again.

David took his expected first, went back to his Sheffield engineering firm immediately, had a hectic trip to America, wrote letters once a week, and came down from the world twice a term to visit her. He refused to attend any college function.

'No.' he said. 'My time's over as far as this place is concerned. Do you know how old I am? Twenty-eight.'

'Poor old man.'

He was right, and she knew it. When he changed firms, they became engaged, and he spent six months in West Africa. As soon as she graduated, he wanted to marry, but she refused until she had done teacher-training. By that time he had accepted a managerial post in London, and there they had set up house. She took a job in a grammar school, enjoyed herself, but left at the end of three terms since she was pregnant with Miranda. It was clear now that her husband had no intention of remaining a practical engineer, was rapidly setting himself up into a directorial rôle. He worked long hours, spent time away; his wife's beauty did him no harm. They moved to a larger house at the firm's expense when Miranda was born, and just when he seemed to be suceeding most brilliantly as an entrepreneur, he applied, or was talked into, a post in a huge, long-established chemical engineering concern in the Midlands. She was surprised, said so. He carefully offered his reasons for change. Again, as when he'd sketched the plan of his studies at university, she was impressed and frightened.

'It scares me,' she said. She did not sound so, and he would not laugh her objections off. He described the solidity, the size, the resources of his new firm, and the very grounds he now praised were the opposites of those he'd flashed a year back. He saw these factories, these congeries of workshops as arenas for his performance. Within two more years he was promoted again, and twelve months later, after considerable commercial successes in the Far East, he moved the family to their present residence. He'd made his high mark, but she thought his friends outnumbered enemies. Colleagues envied, but saw him as different from themselves. He behaved as pleasantly as possible, but when he acted, or argued, or issued orders, speed disguised tremendous weight.

She was expected to open her house to his fellow-directors, and this she did with success. They did not exactly wish Watson's wife to be either southern or cultured; that she was beautiful, well dressed and tactful made her dinner parties popular, her social life full. Nannies and an *au pair* girl helped with Miranda, but the mother spent sufficient time with the child to assuage guilt. Occasionally she found herself bored at functions, and often she realized that men whose names appeared on the front pages of national newspapers as well as on the lists of directors of important concerns (or in the Cabinet), were no match for her husband in energy or creative talent. Twice or three times when David had outlined his plans to her, the differences between the original conception and his final 'proposals for consideration' were staggering. He never raised the flat, northern voice, but she could not be struck by the constant dazzle of new ideas and objections and solutions. His very modesty of approach emphasized his, she did not baulk at the word, genius.

Since their move here she'd been thoroughly occupied, furnishing the new house, helping in the extensive garden, entertaining, visiting, and since John Watson's heart attack spending days in the stuffy semi in Sheffield. She'd joined a film society, went regularly to theatres and concerts, more often than not on her own, or with women friends, as David could not spare the time. And so far this had seemed satis-factory, because when her husband did come home, he appre-

ciated the place, complimented her on it, took pleasure in her
meals, her arrangements, played with and instructed his
daughter, thanked Liz genuinely for the efforts she expended
on his father. He was generous with money, and, often as she
wished, took her abroad for short trips, made lavish provision
for their holidays. She wished that he arrived back at five-
thirty each evening and had the whole of Saturday and
Sunday at home week in, week out, but she had accepted the
inevitable. As she'd put up with, approved even, one evening
a week of his company they'd had when he was driving on for
his first at the university, so now. David Watson was a remarkable man; she'd occupy herself and not hinder him.
She'd known what to expect.

Sometimes she'd wonder how she'd feel in ten years' time.
At half-past eight this evening David came down, still in
his lunching-out suit, and demanded a word with her.

3

She waved her arms, indicating that this place had its advantages for a conference, but he suggested they should go to
his study.

'If you want to talk, I'll go out,' John Watson said.

'There's no need for that,' his son answered. The huffy
look on his father's face implied that there was urgent need
for communication, but no more was said as she meekly made
for the door.

He followed her upstairs, but forced her to wait as he
unlocked his room. He ushered her in, hung back while
she chose a chair. Outside the window facing west the sky
gleamed; she sat with her back to it. He advanced to his
desk and switched on lights before confronting her, carefully

crossing his legs. She watched the operation. He coughed, dug his chin into his collar.

'The Gill Paige business is off,' he said.

She looked at her shoes, did not feel called on to comment.

'We met today, and talked. We're not going through with it.'

Again he paused, allowing her a chance she did not take. 'I realize the distress I must have caused you by my premature announcement. We had made our minds up, and I thought it only honest to tell you. Now we've changed them.' He put words together well, she thought; they sounded sincere and impressive. She wished to find them bogus, but could not. 'I don't know what difference this will make to you, and I don't suppose I've any right to ask.' He put his head on one side; she did not look. 'But there's Miranda. We should have had to come to some agreement about her in any case. I intended to try to discuss it with you. Would you like a drink?'

She shook her head. He poured himself whisky from a squared decanter, sipped.

'I can also see quite clearly that I am in no position to bargain with you. I acted badly, very badly. I can't expect much from you.' Again the courteous pause. When again she took no advantage of it, he showed no displeasure, merely moving his whisky glass a few inches along the opened flap of his desk. 'What I'd like to propose now is that we postpone further discussion and when we have had the opportunity . . .' He waved the rest of the sentence away. 'As you can imagine I am, well, disturbed about what I've done. To you and Miranda primarily. But to myself, and, to some extent, to Gill. But I'd be grateful if you'd agree to say no more for the moment, to take no decision.'

He waited, watching her.

At his first announcement this evening, she had felt a stab of gladness because she had never contemplated any fracture in their marriage before that earlier, shattering statement. It had been her ignorance which had buffeted her so violently. She ought to have suspected, but had not; to have seen, but had failed to do so. Now she had him at a disadvantage, she wished to make something of it.

'Is that agreed, then?'

When he spoke his voice had no tremor; he was at ease. No wonder he did so well at business when he could sit with his fine suit uncreased. He would not, she thought, have decided to live with Mrs Paige on impulse; he'd have considered a hundred possibilities. Nor was it likely that he'd changed his mind at the last minute. Therefore, it must have been Gill, and if that were so, he would feel like death, his *amour propre* in tatters, and yet he spoke as steadily, not a breath misplaced, as if he were reading Miranda a bedtime verse. She looked him over; immaculate, watching her in return.

'Do you agree?' he asked without exasperation.

'Why aren't you . . . why aren't you?' She hardly recognized her voice.

'Look, I'd prefer to talk about that some other time.'

'What did she say?'

He lifted his glass to his lips, buying time.

'I owe you something,' he said. 'I owe you a great deal. And if in a day or two you want a full account still, I'll do my best. But not now, if you don't mind.'

'You need to rehearse it?'

'I need something.' But his voice was true, steady; his hand relaxed at the glass. 'I'm sorry, Liz. You can't imagine what a cock-up this is for me.'

She rose; now was the time to leave him.

'You've not done me any good.' She could not resist it.

'So I imagine.'

'What does your father know about it?'

'Nothing.'

32

'You hadn't told him you were going?'

'No.'

'That was for me, was it? I had to break the news?'

'I'm sorry. I didn't want to worry him more than or sooner than was necessary.' More than, sooner than; the words rang in her head.

'So you won't say anything now?'

'Probably not,' he said.

'You realize he's worrying already?'

'Yes. Don't make it worse for him.'

'And if I do?'

'I'm uttering no threats.' He managed a smile on that, a smooth bastard.

She paused, keeping him frozen in his chair, before she walked, head high, to the door. She opened it without trouble, closed it noiselessly. As soon as she was outside her legs trembled violently so that she shuffled her way to the banister, and downstairs one painful tread at a time. He did not emerge, so that she reached the kitchen undisturbed, turned on the electric kettle, slumped on a stool, elbows on the working surface. The whistle surprised her; the thing could not boil inside seconds. The reaching for instant coffee, stirring it was a major enterprise. She'd have to move for milk.

This would not do.

She forced herself into the sitting-room to ask John Watson if he wanted a cup. When she returned the old man pulled his glasses down his nose, then removed them.

'I like these mugs,' he said. She gave a brief account of their provenance as he pursed his lips and sucked the coffee. He resembled his son, but in a gentler mould. He looked at life from round corners. 'Are you and milord getting on all right?' he asked.

'Yes.' She waited. 'There's been a difference,' she could smile, 'but we're resolving it.'

'Ah. I'm glad. It's him, isn't it? Not you, I mean, who's fed up.'

'Yes. But it's settled now.'

'They talk,' he tapped the *Listener* on his knee, 'about the seven-year itch.'

'We've done nearly eight.'

He smiled, and his face grew wrinkled, perfect. He'd have been better looking than David in his youth, less rough hewn.

'Well, it's a good job you can joke about it, that's all I can say.' He replaced his spectacles. 'You're very comfortable here, but that's not everything. You know, Elizabeth, I can talk to you a lot easier than I can to him.'

'That's good.'

He resumed his reading, shy.

David went back to his office on Tuesday morning, but without hurrying, making himself pleasant over breakfast to his father, chattering to Miranda, helping with the dishes so that it was nine-thirty before he left the house. Miranda and grandfather accompanied him to the garage, where they shouted and waved excitedly. Liz watched upstairs. At mid-day he telephoned to say he'd be home for dinner at six.

Elizabeth took her two out in the car that afternoon. She and Miranda chased about the park, watched the police training their horses, crept up close to the deer. Watson, stumping not far from the car, got into conversation with an old passenger-guard, and enjoyed himself.

'Wesleyan Methodist,' he reported to his daughter-in-law.

'Isn't that so good?'

'They were a cut above us, so they thought. We're all the same now, of course; have been for forty-odd years.'

'But they haven't noticed?'

'Elizabeth.' He shook his finger, delighted, but could not bring himself to call her 'Liz'. His irony, his clarity of vision was all-pervasive, but practically affected only small areas of his life. He noted the pretension of his co-religionists, their ridiculous hypocrisies, but his faith remained firm. 'What would they be like if they didn't attend chapel?' he'd ask his son. 'And for that matter, what should I be like? I'm not one to talk.'

'Elizabeth.' Now Miranda imitated him, in admiration.

'He used to take the old fasts up to London, and he met some rum people. Made me laugh. Treated main-line expresses as if they were local taxis, some of them. We didn't get any of that up at the front end.'

'I thought dukes tipped the drivers.'

When they arrived home Miranda and John reached down books to identify the park deer. David arrived exactly on time, acted comfortably through dinner, read to Miranda, and then as the evening before asked to speak to his wife.

'Conference every night,' John Watson commented.

'Better than not speaking,' Liz, generously.

'I shall be having a word with you next, my man.' David much at his ease. 'In half an hour, then. I'd like to write and post a letter.'

'Won't be collected till morning.' Father, siding with the woman.

Elizabeth knitted, and looked at the television screen. She heard her husband go out and return ten minutes later. He made a phone call, from the annexe, not from his study. When he came in he wore carpet slippers and a sports coat.

'Are you ready?' he asked.

She bobbed to her father-in-law, who with equal irony inclined his head. Upstairs, she again took the same chair as on the previous night, moving it to suit herself, back to the light. 'Drink?'

'No, thank you.' He helped himself.

'I have to apologize again,' he began. 'Sincerely. I realize it makes no difference, but I want you to understand that I know how you must feel.' He'd prepared that. 'I can't possibly amend what I've done.' Right word? 'I can say how

35

sorry I am, however inadequate that is, and that's all. But we have to go on, Liz. One way or the other. You see that?'

She saw nothing, wishing she had accepted a drink.

'I went to Bill Whittaker's for lunch, and then met Gill in the afternoon.'

'Where?'

'I picked her up, and we drove out to Papplewick. We talked in the car. We decided we were not going on with our plan.'

'Why?'

'You. Miranda. Tony. There was too much complication.'

'Who decided?'

'I did.' No hesitation. 'But it was what she wanted.'

'Hadn't you gone into all that before? Where were you to live together? In a hotel?'

'For a start, yes. I'd got a house more or less laid on.'

'Where?' What did it matter?

'The Park. Newcastle Drive. New link house.'

'Go on, then.' She'd not leave him alone.

'We decided not to. It was painful. But once I'd made my mind up I knew I'd done right. It's the consequences we have to consider now.' He smiled in a grim, squinting way. 'I've got to hear what you're prepared to do.'

'Presumably you were in love with her?' Vinegary voice prim. 'With Mrs Paige?'

'Yes.'

'Are you still?'

'I find that very difficult to answer. I was sufficiently attracted to Gill to want to live with her. It was strong as that. I don't want you to underestimate . . .'

'How long has this been going on?'

'Two months.'

'Is that all?' She showed her contempt.

'Are you prepared to have me back?' he said, then waited. 'That's the first question. You've had a few hours to mull it over.' He grimaced at his cliché. 'But we shall have to come down before too long, on one side or the other.'

'You mean, "Do I want a divorce?" '

'That's a possibility, certainly,' he said.

They paused, and she found the silence hostile.

'Do you know what strikes me?' she asked.

'Go on.'

'You're very cool about all this.' He ventured nothing. 'When you met Gill Paige that afternoon, did you know you were going to break it off?'

'No. Not exactly. But it seemed worth broaching.' His constant discussions with lawyers had given him words.

'And she jumped at the chance?'

'Look.' He seemed weary rather than exasperated. 'If you like to think of it like that, that's up to you. It wasn't so, but I'm not here to discuss Gill.'

'Doesn't that make a difference?' she asked.

'Maybe. But you'll have to make up your mind without information on that score. I've been a bloody fool. If I heard of somebody else acting so, I wouldn't have much to say in his favour. I don't expect you to go out of your way to accommodate me.'

'Not much of a basis for marriage?' she prodded.

'I don't know. There's Miranda. But it's up to you.'

'What do you want?'

'To come back. I've told you.'

'And you want your answer now?'

'Not of necessity. But I'm not prepared to wait too long.'

'Would you prefer,' she spoke civilly, 'just at this moment to live with Mrs Paige rather than with me?'

'I don't know. I can't answer that. As soon as we'd decided, the perspective was changed. That sounds daft, makes it seem we weren't serious, but that's how it was. If she rang up to say she'd changed her mind again, I'd disappoint her.'

'You'll be seeing her, though?'

'We didn't say. In the furore.' He smiled. 'The break made one hell of a difference.'

'Had she told her husband?'

'No, she hadn't.'

'Why did you come out with it to me?' she asked.

'It seemed honest.'

'My God.'

The conversation engaged only the crust of her mind, a temperate zone, unaffected as yet by the violence of fire underneath. She could talk without harm to herself; she wished to wound him, but calmly. There must be more. There ought to be.

'Well, what do you say, then?' he began, steadily.

'Nothing.'

'What does that mean?'

'What it says. You'll have to wait for me, now.'

'Within reason.' A threat?

'I don't know about that. You don't seem to see what you've done. You announce you're deserting me, and incidentally your daughter and your father, and when you come back you're not quite sure whether you're going to continue your affair. What do you think this has done to me? I can never trust you again. Let's say we patch this up, what's the next bit of fancywork you'll be on with?'

'You want a divorce?'

'I don't want bloody anything. You, or your family, or your whisky. I don't want anything.' She was crying, in a detached way; feverish as if she'd run hard, she did not mind the discomfort. 'I don't want you.'

'I can understand that,' he said.

'Understand, understand? You've done this to me. Without thinking. In honesty. "I'm going to leave you." That's what you said. "I'm going to leave you." That's all I mean now. Somebody you're going to leave. "I'm going to leave you." '

He watched her with compassion perhaps, or shame. She continued, headlong.

'You're mad. To think you can say that, and nothing happens. You're not sane; you're not human. Two or three days ago, you'd done with me, you'd turned me out. Now you're back, asking me what I want. Do you expect me to forget?'

'No.'

'No. Is that all you can say? No? You alter every single . . . It's useless talking. You've no idea what you've done. I'm a human being.'

'I didn't think otherwise.'

The courteous, northern voice riled; presumably he was making soothing noises, but he suggested mild sarcasm to her.

'Go away,' she said, tears running. 'I don't want to have anything to do with you.'

'Are you serious?' he asked.

'Yes. It's finished. You finished it off.'

He sighed, massaging his leg above his left knee.

'That's not so,' he answered. 'You and I might never speak to each other again. But there's Miranda. And some financial arrangement will have to be made for you.'

'I'll get a job.'

'That will take time. And jobs are scarce, if you're thinking about teaching.'

'I'll work in a shop or a factory.'

'I expect you will,' he answered, 'but until you do, I have some responsibility. And it's no use rushing into things you'll regret just because you feel as you do now. I'll say again how sorry I am. I'll say again, whether you believe it or not, that I'll do anything I can to make up for . . . for what's happened. And we'd better leave it there.'

'How can we?'

'I'm not asking for forgiveness. What I'm suggesting is

that you'd do better to wait until you see this in a different light, and then . . . .'

'Can't I see it now?'

'No, Liz, with respect, you can't. You're sore, confused, not yourself. I don't blame you. It's my fault. All I'm saying is, "Give yourself a few days' grace." '

'What you mean is that it'll be better for you, then.'

'For both, I hope.'

'What do you care? About me? You deserted me.'

'Yes,' he said. 'But I should have made financial provision. You wouldn't have been left to fend for yourself.'

'You can afford two wives, can you?'

'I'm doing my best to keep my head. But don't go on too long. Any insult you can think up about me I've thought for myself. I might be seven sorts of despicable bastard, and I don't mind your saying so. I welcome it. I don't want you festering there. But I'm warning you I can only stand so much.'

'And what about me, then?'

He did not answer, but swung his arms to clasp hands with a small smack behind his chair. His position, both awkward and relaxed, taunted her. She no longer wept, but her body consisted of hard centres of pain, chest, shoulders, upper arms, face backbone, hips; so conscious was she of this discomfort that she began to lose sight of her husband. Her distress solidified, or shifted, inside her self and occupied her fully. She did not seek for causes, bear grudges, even.

She got to her feet.

'You let me know,' he said. 'When you're ready.'

'I will.' A childish retort.

'Thanks for listening to me. I don't deserve it.'

This did not seem like her husband, but rather some dummy with a speaking voice. She had made love with this man, seen him in anxiety, laughed with him in mutual pleasure. Now he said the correct sentence, even touched with

40

flashes of temper, but he wasn't human. As she moved she half expected him to leap up to open the door, to bend flunkey-wise as she passed. He sat there, holding his limbs still, not touching his glass.

She went straight downstairs, not bothering to examine her face.

John Watson nodded vigorously, pulling his face into a smile as she entered.

'Conference over?' he said, peering.

'Yes.' She sat down, picked up a library book. 'Don't you want the telly?'

'No, thanks. Is everything all right? Upstairs?'

'Well.' She drawled the word out, comically, she hoped.

'It isn't. But will it be?' he suggested.

'Something like that.'

'I'm not going to interrogate you,' he said. 'You've got your work cut out. He can be awkward, can our David. But I expect you knew that when you married him. I often wish you'd met Annie, his mother. She was like him. Had a lot of spare energy. Couldn't understand how a man could be satisfied going through life as an engine driver. Wouldn't exactly say so. Let you know, though, without speaking. And there he was. Insisted on leaving school after his "A" levels. She didn't like it. But.' He blew breath out, feebly, and spread his fingers.

'Are you feeling ... ?'

'Yes, yes.' Davidian impatience. 'These days, by eight or nine o'clock, I'm ready for bed. I can hardly believe it. At lunch time I'm as lively as ever I've been, but I droop. I look forward from six o'clock onwards to getting into the warm sheets. It's a waste of life.'

'I don't know.'

'What, whacked, doing nothing?'

'At least,' she said. 'You don't get into trouble.'

4

Three or four days later David presided at conferences abroad, but rang home politely from Stuttgart, from Düsseldorf, reporting his movements. He made no inquiries about her intentions.

On the Saturday morning she had finished breakfast when the phone disturbed her preparations of lists in the kitchen.

'Good morning. Mrs Watson? You won't know me, but my name is Anthony Paige. I don't think we've met.' He'd taken it for granted she would place him. 'I'm sorry to trouble you at this time in the morning, but I'd be grateful if you'd allow me to come to see you. It won't take up much of your time.'

She inquired, drily, for the reason.

'I don't want to say too much on the phone. It's about my wife. Gill. You've met her.'

'When?' She cut him short.

'This morning? Would it be possible? It won't take long.' No. This gushing school prefect would straighten his face and ask what she intended to do about her husband's adultery with his wife. She'd no idea what he expected of her. To conspire? To condone, as they comforted each other? It sounded askew.

'Eleven o'clock.' She consulted her wristwatch, and he volleyed his thanks.

When she returned from her shopping, she tried to compose herself. During these last few days she had lacked qualms, surprised by her conviction that if she sat quietly all would be well, by the absence of hate for her husband. Now this man would disturb, stir, spoil.

His appearance jolted her: he was not so young as she had imagined, was wrinkled about the eyes, dry-skinned. His grey hair was stylishly cut, but his shirt clashed too garish for her taste. He shook hands firmly, repeated his name, said that she was very good to see him, and, many thanks, he would have a cup of coffee. She led him to an armchair, and when she came back, he sat exactly as she had left him, right leg over left, right hand spread on knee. He rose, but did not hover. She offered commonplaces about the weather, the spring, the garden, determined to be civilized. He smiled, made no attempt to push conversation, but on his first sip of coffee, he returned his cup to the table and began.

'It's very kind of you to have me, Mrs Watson, very kind. And I don't want to take up too much of your time, but I thought this was sufficient of an emergency to warrant my presumption.' She examined his suit, excellent lightweight, light grey material. 'It's about my wife, Gill.' Elizabeth sat straighter. 'I don't know how well you know her. You have met, I realize.'

Elizabeth murmured deprecatingly.

'You had perhaps gathered that she has had one quite serious breakdown?' Who'd begin like that?

'No.'

'Some seven years ago. We had been married only comparatively a short time, a matter of two years. She had in fact to be . . . to go into hospital. Not for long. A little less than a month.'

That handsome, striking firebrand of a woman, her rival, who had chidden David publicly for carelessness about the fate of vivisected animals, that goddess of the bunglers who had been surrounded by men she made appear insignificant by the strength of her convictions and her high colour, blue-black hair, great, dark eyes. Elizabeth wondered if David knew they had put his beloved away into a lunatic asylum.

'I see.' She did not.

'Since she met you and your husband she's, and I'm speaking literally, not allowed a day to pass without mentioning you. It's remarkable. She's not a woman who's easily impressed. I know that people think if you've had mental trouble you chase straws, have no control, and I suppose there's truth in that. But, if anybody does, she lacks the bump,' he giggled slightly, 'of adulation. She did not fall in love with her psychiatrist, attractive as he might be; she would have done better, perhaps, if she had. But with you and your husband, especially you, it is as if the dam's given way.'

Elizabeth looked aside; he tested her, she thought, cruelly. When she had nodded sufficiently, piled up a half-dozen affirmatives, he'd rap her sharply with 'They're lovers', scoring over her, getting some vulgar fraction of his own back.

'Now this is why I have come to you. You're busy, I know. I don't want you to waste your time. Would you see her?'

'See? I don't quite ...'

'I'm afraid. She's losing her stability. She's consulting doctors. The specialist as well as our man said: "Hasn't she got some woman friend she can confide in?", and the answer is that she hasn't. She's a powerful personality. She likes her own ... She's self-centred. She doesn't tread warily, and is likely to blurt out exactly what she thinks. This is not the way to keep friends. I'm speaking frankly, Mrs Watson. I feel I owe you that. Gill has many good qualities, as you'd find out. But. She tramples.' His face closely shaved, glowed with health, well-being. 'I'm desperate, I can tell you. And I've no idea whether this will do any good. But she admires you, in a fashion I have never noticed ....'

'She hardly knows me.'

'That's true. But she would like to cultivate the acquaintance.'

Elizabeth turned her head away from the periphrasis.

'She might soon think otherwise, if she did get to know me.'

'We could try. I am asking you if ... I don't ...' He shook his head, blowing out breath, preparing to weep, she thought.

'Wouldn't she resent the fact that I've been forced on her?'

'Again she might. Could we try? Would you? It's asking a good deal, I know. Why should you entangle yourself with an unbalanced, demanding woman? It's a shot in the dark.'

'There are no other friends you can think of?'

'No. I've thought this through. There are not.'

He seemed suddenly to remember his coffee, to be delighted at the recollection, so that his expression changed as he reached out, curved cup and saucer in towards himself like a slow-motion version of the initial movement of a courtly bow. She distrusted him, it, waited. Now he was in no hurry.

'What do you say, then?' Right hand clasped chin; blue eyes widened, fastened on hers.

'Just spell it out for me.' She avoided rudeness. 'Please.'

'I suggest that the pair of you meet.'

'How?'

'I don't understand you,' he said, lofty forehead barely crinkling.

'I can't just ring your wife and say, "Look, let's be friends." '

'It would be marvellous if you could.'

She shook her head, hardly believing that this man, this polished self-creation, was ignorant of his wife's infidelity.

'What would you suggest?' He showed eagerness. 'I'm willing to try anything. That is, if you are prepared to meet her.'

'It seems so unlikely. That I can ...'

'Help a desperate woman ... ?'

'To think that I can. It sounds like fantasy.'

'On my part?' he asked.

'Yes. I appreciate your anxiety over your wife's condition. But there's no evidence that I shall have the slightest effect on her.'

45

'There's no evidence,' he said, speaking sternly, steadily, 'that anything anybody will do will cure her. But I must try. The doctors suggest she needs a friend. You,' again he mouthed a smile, 'seem to fit the bill. She'll be under treatment from the hospital. She already is. But I must do everything I can. You see that.'

Elizabeth licked her lips, unable to believe still that this was anything except a prelude to the announcement of adultery. Anthony Paige leaned towards her, in appeal. She felt he might stretch his hands out at any minute, drop to his knees. Ridiculous.

'Look,' she said. The word warned. 'I've no experience. I suppose I'm flattered, but I can't help thinking your trust is misplaced.' He uncurled his fingers towards her. 'I'm willing to give it a try, though, if that's what you want.'

'Thank you, Mrs Watson. You don't . . .'

'You tell her what you've suggested. I've no time for secrecy and play-acting.' She did not know why she said that. 'She must realize she's trying me out as a confidante, and then if she doesn't like it, well. So you must tell her. And she must ring me and arrange a meeting.'

'I don't think that she'll do that.'

'Why not?' She relented. 'I'll ring her, then, after you've explained what you've done.'

'I thought perhaps we should give an appearance, or try, of an accidental meeting. Chance, you know.'

'No. You talk to her, tell me when you've done so, and I'll get in touch.'

He sat uneasily, twitched his shoulders, but said no more until he had finished his coffee, when he thanked her, cordially now, said he'd take up no more of her time, and left, with a knowledgeable remark or two on the garden. A faint tang of his aftershave hung in the room; she did not like him. As soon as she began to examine her unfavourable reaction, she realized that it had no rationality behind it. She disliked his shirt, his smart appearance; he epitomized the business executive of a television serial; his interference in her life, his gratuitous handing-out of difficult, unpaid, uninteresting work was impertinent. She did not trust him, because she did not believe he was ignorant of his wife's infidelity. Worst, he had probed the stinking wound of her pride. She'd been about to compromise, had prepared herself to do nothing, eat valium, for a fortnight or a month until she could bear what her husband had done to her, but this man had made it impossible in his fashionable suit and shining car.

At four o'clock he phoned to say he had fulfilled his part of the bargain. She promised to ring Gillian on Sunday afternoon.

David was back, with acceptable, not expensive presents for her and Miranda, a chess-set for the child, a nest of jasper eggs for her. The Sunday lunch was traditional and a success, roast beef and a blackberry and apple pudding which father-in-law praised.

'That's the best suet pudding I've ever tasted,' he said.

'In all your life?' Miranda asked.

'In all my life, I tell you. And you know what I think about pips.'

Miranda crowed as if she believed; Elizabeth, who had spent the morning constructing sentences for Gill Paige as she cooked, knew joy. David, replete without a second help-ing, piled the dishes into the machine, and offered to drive the party out after grandfather had slept over his cup of tea. At three, Elizabeth packed the two men, Miranda, Anna-Lise the *au pair* girl, off, and stared sourly at the telephone. She walked upstairs, cleaned her teeth, changed her shoes, sat on her bed in a vagueness of displeasure. She had not yet moved back into the main bedroom, and sullenly occupied herself now wondering how she would answer a request from David for her return.

The house stood hugely silent; a shower lashed the double-glazed windows of a sudden, so that fat drops hung, coalesced, sagging into streams. She pulled her mouth awry; she'd better get the phone call over, before rain drove the family back.

Even so, she stood in hesitation before she dialled. She had been badly caught out by Paige's appeal, because she expected something worse. Not now was she sure of the man. She drew up a chair, announced herself.

'Gill Paige here.' That sounded sane enough.

'Your husband came to see me and suggested we met. Does that make sense to you?'

'It's kind of you. I don't know how to thank you.'

'When can we . . . ?'

'As soon as you please.'

'Would you like to come here?' Liz asked, 'or shall I call at your place? I have a car.'

'I don't like either. There are reasons, really, against both, but you must excuse me if I don't . . . This must all sound foolish to you. Or perhaps it's what you expect, is it? From what Tony told you?'

'No, not at all.'

'Will you suggest somewhere? And a time.'

'Tomorrow afternoon. Three o'clock. The Castle.' Elizabeth was pleased with that; sharp efficiency. Mrs Paige agreed; conversation died on them, budded briefly into thanks.

On Monday, Elizabeth stood there first, straight, waiting outside the gateway, one eye suspiciously on a threatening sky. Gill Paige, walking, was on her almost before she noticed, chiefly because she had expected something more flamboyant than the navy coat with silver buttons, the hatless head.

'Am I late? I came on the bus. It's not really safe to drive while I'm on so many tablets.' The voice struck bright, ordinary, unfrightening. They walked uphill together, but now, with uncertain weather, few people presented themselves. Two children ran screaming. A young man lit his pipe. Among the flowerbeds which paraded neat lines of colour Gill Paige walked breathlessly so that Liz slackened her pace.

'I'm out of condition, you can tell,' Gill said.

'We won't go up the steps, then.'

'Oh, yes, we will. I'll make myself.'

In fact, she had no difficulty. They paused at the top to stare over the city, their pleasure ruined by tower-block hospital, hotels, offices, but as they solemnly eyed the flat industrial area by the river a spatter of rain forced them into sharp movements with umbrellas. They quickened their step, two smart ladies, and dashed laughingly through the door, into the foyer, then beyond to the cafeteria. Elizabeth after winning an argument, fetched coffee for herself, orange for Gill. Drink looks unappetizing in paper cups. They cleared their umbrellas, arranged themselves by a freshly dishclothed table.

'Here we are,' Gill said.

'We are indeed.' Liz's partner, opponent, rival, sat strikingly upright, her blue coat opened Byronically back from the white throat, the sapphire necklet, the purity of blouse. This woman David loved, had loved. Her hair was black, magnificently dark, alive, blue-black, admirably cut, curled, but with a barbarism in its colour, a ferocity. Elegance overlay wildness.

'I expect my husband surprised you,' Gill began, after a respectable moment.

'Well, yes.'

'What exactly did he say? He's a great talker, but I'm never sure where he's been or where he's going. That sounds bad. You tell me.'

'He said that you'd had nervous trouble, and that the doctors had recommended you to talk to some friend. As there was no one, either you or he decided I'd fill the bill.'

'Did you think so?' Rudely, fierce.

'No, I didn't. And said so. But he pressed me, so I've presented myself.'

Gillian eyed her as if she appreciated the choice of vocabulary. She'd met an antagonist, if nothing else, and she'd be wary.

'And how did he, Tony, seem?'

'It's the first time I'd met him.'

'Did he create a favourable impression?' Gill laughed, good teeth bared. 'He'd dress up.'

'I wondered what I'd be like if I had to put such a proposition to a stranger.'

'Don't you think there are people who enjoy putting themselves into such tricky positions, to see if they've the wit to talk themselves out?'

'Probably.'

'You think I'm odd, don't you, to talk of my husband like this? It's embarrassing for me.'

'I can see that.'

Gillian Paige suddenly switched herself off to stare out of the window. Elizabeth, prepared for anything, drank the dregs of her coffee, and looked round at urns, glass cabinets for sandwiches, trays of cups, the bowed attendant going through the motions with her dishcloth. Two other women, elderly and stout, whispered in a far corner. A child and her father came sheepishly in, ordering an ice cream after consultation of a chart. The waitress approved the choice. 'Them's really nice.'

'Shall we walk round?' Gill asked. 'Improve our minds?'

The father eyed them with admiration as his daughter licked.

They walked upstairs, Gillian tapping with her ring on the polished brass handrail. They stood before Blind Homer, Gill in the position of a learned lecturer about to expound.

She nodded to herself as if satisfied, but spoilt it by laughing, though at nothing. They did the round of the Boningtons, Liz leading.

As they stepped through into the large hall, a uniformed attendant smiled, wished them good afternoon.

'Do you see anything you like?' Liz asked.

'I don't. They make me feel uncomfortable.'

'Why's that?'

'They must represent someone's idea of good taste. Some official.'

'Unless they're gifts.'

'They needn't hang everything they're given. It's depressing, isn't it? All this so-called art.'

'There's no compulsion for us to stay,' Liz said.

'Let's go.' Then, pathetically, hands fluttering. 'Where?'

'My daughter likes the mummified cats.'

'No, thank you.' They turned about. 'We aren't doing too well, are we? You don't approve of me. I'm sorry.'

'I hardly know you,' Liz answered.

'That's the trouble. I don't know anybody, anything.' The sentences dropped with hypocritical unction from the elegant mouth, but rang strongly, strangely enough. Now they were clear of the galleries, and skirting the dull walls, beginning to work their way downhill under skies that brightened, with rain no longer a threat.

'It was all very silly, to ask you,' Gill said. 'Well, it was, wasn't it?'

'If you think so.'

'You're less sympathetic on the surface than I thought you would be. Less soft.'

'I've hardly said a word,' Liz objected.

'That's what I mean.'

'I'm sorry.'

They walked along together, stride for stride, and to Liz at least there was something theatrical in the promenade,

51

especially as the grounds stood so empty. Someone had pre-pared an elaborate and empty stage for them, and there they'd act out their nothing. Footsteps clipped strictly; they turned about at the end of the path.

'You know, don't you?' Gill Paige asked, stopping. Liz deliberately continued to walk forward, so that she had time, as she stopped and wheeled.

'Know what?'

'About David and me?'

'Yes.'

The word afforded no inkling of the savage blow that short sentence had lashed across her body.

'He told you?'

'Yes, he did.' The voice steadied itself, worked her work for her.

'So he said. I didn't know whether to believe him. Men usually lie. I wasn't surprised when he announced it was off, though. He was very matter of fact. We sat in his car; he'd been to some business lunch party, and he just came out with it.'

'That's not the way I heard it.'

'Go on, then.'

'I had the impression,' Liz said, 'that it was an agreed thing. Whoever put it into words first is beside the point, he told me. You both knew it was right.'

Gill resumed her pacing. Liz caught up.

'I was never certain.'

'You thought he'd draw back, do you mean?'

'Yes. I'm not sure of anything, but . . . He talked about you, and Miranda, and his father. You've frightened him, haven't you, knocked the hell out of him? It's utterly odd, that somebody like David, a flier, a whizz-kid in business, laying the law down, blasting the pundits, should be such a mouse at home.' She laughed. Liz resented the sound. It was this punctuating cackle rather than her words which limned

the unbalance. 'I pretty well had to drag the trousers off him.'
She sighed now. 'Are you going to take him back?'

'Undecided.'

'Jesus. It doesn't take all that long to find out whether or
not you can put up with him. I'd know by now.'

'You and I are different, then.'

'No wonder you frighten him. You wouldn't hit me, would
you?'

'It never crossed my mind.'

They reached the turnstile by the gate; Liz turned round,
set off back, while Gill scuttled to catch up.

'When my husband phoned you . . .,' she began, alongside,
'you thought he wanted to talk about me and David?'

'That's right.'

'God. And you sat waiting for him to come out with it?
And he never did?' Again the laugh.

'What would he do if he found out?' Liz felt she must
regain some advantage.

'He won't.' The certainty sounded mad. 'If he did, he'd
shout and thump the table, and that would be all.'

'He wouldn't get rid of you?'

'You can be a bastard, can't you? But, no. He wouldn't.
Without me he doesn't know where he is. He looks the part,
doesn't he? Smart man of affairs. But he's a schoolboy still,
shit-scared of his father. He daren't let this break up.'

'If you'd have gone off with David?'

'He'd have been snivelling round, begging me back so that
his father couldn't get at him.'

'He sounds . . .'

'Sounds. He's no David. But he has advantages. There's
money, and comfort. And he looks after me, and doesn't
mind if I kick his crotch in. He's been dominated all his life,
and now he likes it.'

'That's not the way he speaks of you,' Liz said.

'No, I'm the little woman with the nervous ailment who

53

needs wrapping up warm, and caring for, and all the rest of the bullshit.'

'Isn't it true?'

'Do you think David would hitch himself to a woman half-way round the twist?'

'David has never hitched himself to anybody except me.'

'Oh, fuck you, then. Yes, I had a spell in the asylum. I'm not afraid to call it by its proper name.'

'It's no wish of mine to poke into your business . . . ,' – Gill's face set into a frozen laugh which did not sound – '. . . but beds in those places are at a premium. They don't take you in for nothing.'

'There's no need to instruct me. I was bad enough, then. And you want to know why.' Gill Paige shrugged hugely, a scarecrow dropping into constituent sticks and rags, quite inappropriate to the neat, blue suit. 'Chemical imbalance. Something rotten in the noradrenaline. And don't get thinking it was due to something that happened outside. It wasn't. It knocked me over. I hated myself. But it happened.'

'And this was the first time?'

They had walked the end of the path and were now standing looking over the castle wall, to the streets below, the neat warehouses, the industrial museum, the oldest inn in England, though neither saw a brick or the dart of a bird. Gill pushed on the stones with one hand, while Liz clasped hers in front. Both women were caught up in the conversation, locked inside it, not very aware of the other, except as a cause of the maelstrom.

'Yes. No. This was the worst. I'd been depressed and treated by doctors. But never shut inside. This bombed me. The others were pinpricks.'

'And,' Liz searched for a question, 'it had nothing to do with your marriage.'

'It had. It must have. Suppose you were a mountaineer and started climbing down the cliff here, and your legs suddenly lost all use, well, it would have something to do with the descent, wouldn't it? Chiefly, that you couldn't do it, that you'd have fallen and broken your bloody neck. I was unhappy, or unsettled. It didn't give me what I'd expected. I was restless. But that didn't account for the violence, the severity of the attack.'

'Weren't you afraid that leaving your husband would bring on . . . ?'

'I'm afraid. Yes.' Now Gill moved, indicating the way back. 'You're good at cross-examination, aren't you?'

'It's what I'm here for.' Liz set off.

'I don't know whether this'll be any use. You're hard. Still, I don't mind domineering characters, within limits. You might get worse.'

'It's up to you. You can call it a day any time you like.'

'Is that it? The end?'

'If you wish. Do you want to go back home now? I've got my car, and it won't be out of my way.'

They made their return to the castle gate, where two attendants blocked the door of the office to observe the interesting departure. Little was said, apart from directions, but they sat friendly enough together.

'You're a good driver,' Gill ventured. They were parked under a heavy lime tree. All that could be seen of the Paiges' house was a wide, white-painted wrought-iron gate and thirty straight yards of drive between shrubbery. 'I'm in too much of a hurry. I told you Tony suffered from his father; mine was worse. Was? Is.'

Elizabeth hummed sympathetically.

'My father is a writer. Roderick Wincanton.'

'I've read his book about Thailand, the East. And his novels. When I was at the university I was very taken with *A Negligent Man*. I remember recommending it to the prof.'

'The teachers at my school read him.'

'What's he like? Overpowering?'

'Everything he shouldn't be. And less successful than his deserts, he thinks, so he took it out of me and my mother.'

Gillian fell into silence, a savage concentration on her shoes, which lasted for minutes. Suddenly she shook herself, thanked Liz brightly, said she was grateful, and attempted to leave the car, an effort spoilt by fumbling at the wrong handle. Liz issued an instruction, and Gill, in the street, swung the door in as if she wished to thump it buckled off its hinges, before raising one finger and striding for her drive.

Elizabeth drove off, but stopped two streets away, in a tree-bordered emptiness. She felt herself not so much troubled, as dirtied. The contact had been humdrum enough, but the forceful sentences with their mitigating questions, the screech of unwanted laughter, the confessions, the boasting had impressed her as symptoms of serious maladjustment. Gill Paige and life at odds, a ringside report. She felt her wisest course would be to break off now, refuse further meeting, but she was curious. She remembered a lecture by Sir Roderick Wincanton she had attended, a great performance, all argued with flair, delivered with drama. A handsome man, she recalled, with bushy sidewhiskers and a waxen-ruddy face who had dealt with an audience of two or more hundred as a practised schoolmaster with a half-dozen scruffs. They knew their place, he his. If they did not he soon pointed it out. He disposed of questioners with godlike antitheses, flattering but threatening, warning of the limits of his tolerance of ignorance or stupidity. The middle-aged ladies who made up the bulk of his listeners had gone away edified; if not God, they had seen Moses. Elizabeth tried to recall the topic, but could not. Keats, was it? A sensibility reviewed? That sounded likely, but she was not sure. She remembered his hands on the lectern, the curve of his waistcoat, the reverberating voice swerving into incisive sourness. But she could not fetch back one word. Conrad, was it? Yeats, the

voice of modern rhetoric? A novel for the train? Nothing.
A reed shaken by the wind.

She ought to laugh at her own antics, a Gill-like cackle.

5

When David asked Elizabeth to return to his bed and bedroom, she complied without fuss.

He flew her for two days to Zürich, where in weather
bright as a high summer, she sat staring dizzily by the lake.
At night, they ate and drank, at great cost, stayed up late,
made love. Utterly attentive, he did not appear quite at his
ease, and tried to question her obliquely.

'It would be nice to have Miranda here,' he said.

'Yes, it would.'

'You didn't suggest it.'

'She'd have to miss school.'

What he wanted, she knew, was some indication that she
was satisfied, that he did her proud, that he was making up.
She did not provide it, or at least only ambiguously, saying
the weather was perfect and the Chagals worth the journey.
He had no control over the former, and looked uneasy about
the latter. She smiled, suggesting they ought to have come
for the *Sechseläuten*, only just over. He did not argue, but
narrowed his eyes.

Miranda nearly drove her mad with the musical box they
brought her; it tinkled at six in the morning, would bell its
boring tune at any hour or place. The child was fascinated;
David lectured his daughter on the mechanism, the tiny
spiked barrel, the row of metal rods and though the explanation was clarity itself, the girl pestered him until he fetched
a screwdriver, dismantled the thing, explained and pointed.
When his wife asked if he could put it together again, he

57

showed no impatience, touched the pieces with his finger-nails to demonstrate how well made it was, claiming one would have no difficulty with such workmanship and materials. He was right.

Miranda said slyly, 'Perhaps Mummy wants you to break it.'

'Why would she want that?'

'Because she thinks I play it too much.'

'And do you?'

'Yes. It makes a beautiful sound. Like high-up water.'

She looked carefully at her mother before she moved off with her reassembled box.

'Somebody's sharp,' said John Watson. Elizabeth savoured her daughter's phrase, 'high-up water', and wondered how long it would be before the child grew too embarrassed to coin and come out with such poeticisms.

She received a letter of thanks from Tony Paige, written at length and suggesting that the interview with his wife had been reported, discussed in detail and found satisfactory. Two days later Gill herself rang to invite Liz and David to dinner, to meet her father. 'You did say you liked his books. Most people have never heard of them. If you show him you've read one, he'll be delighted. He eats praise.' She went on to explain that she had phoned first before Tony sent a formal invitation. 'In view of what has happened, I thought perhaps . . .' Liz granted permission, felt a slight disappointment that she could do so without qualms.

The letter was on the breakfast table next morning. David read it and as he passed it across arched his eyebrows, hinting presumably this needed consideration in private. It was innocuous enough, friendly; it said Gill had talked it over with Elizabeth.

'I didn't know you were that well acquainted with her,' he said. He beckoned her outside, had started the conversation without unlocking the car, never mind throwing briefcase on the back seat.

'Well, I am.'

'And you talked, talked, together?'

'We did.' She grinned silently. 'Her husband knows nothing of the aberration. She wants us to meet her father, Roderick Wincanton.' The name clearly meant nothing; this slightly riled him.

'And are we going?'

'Don't see why not.'

'You'll reply, then, will you?'

'No. You will.'

He unlocked the car at that, but paused to kiss Miranda who had come shouting and running towards them.

'Don't go without me,' the girl admonished. Elizabeth immediately followed her daughter indoors, though she was certain David would have appreciated another word. She had no wish to harm him, only to demonstrate that he had no prerogative of surprises.

For his part, he asked nothing more in the next days, and she, reading this as a puritanical penance for his adultery, was glad.

Sir Roderick was less impressive at eye-level than on stage. His suit seemed shabby compared with Tony's or David's, and had not been good in the first place. He spent a lot of his time in heavy, uncomfortable breathing, almost panting, and he shook hands feebly. The mane of hair was thinner than one expected, and the face more pouched, sagging, shapeless; he might have been an ugly, middle-aged woman. They drank sherry and martinis, and Gill looked sparklingly attractive, in contrast with her father who complained that his heart did not allow him to drink. When Liz pressed him on his ailments, he seemed unwilling to offer more than a few asthmatic grouses, though his jacket reeked of tobacco. He sat depressed, unprepared to break out of himself.

Tony's parents arrived to make up the party. Both were

small, but the father laid down the law, if pleasantly, in a deep Yorkshire voice. The accent was more pronounced than David's, so strong as to seem cultivated, and the voice powerful for a man of his size. Jovial enough to the rest, he had obviously met Wincanton before and disliked him. He talked knowledgeably to David about business matters, and once contradicted him; his blue eyes opened wide for a moment when the younger man flattened his assertion with a few, curt facts. For the rest of the time before dinner he became subdued.

The meal passed pleasantly and leisurely, the host and hostess serving. Gill enjoyed cooking, but plainly. She said so, and claimed she dared cook in no other way when Phil and Eileen Paige dined with them. Her mother-in-law raised protesting squawks, but the old man said beef tasted good enough without wine splashed all over it, especially boiled wine. He'd do his own splashing if they didn't mind. Once or twice Liz tried to draw Wincanton about Thailand, but he muttered and fumbled at his food, as if he were half-witted. What he said, for instance, about the learning of eastern languages was interesting, but delivered monotonously, gutlessly, mind caught up on some barbed wire elsewhere. He ate heartily enough, but with sighing wheezes, and put down his utensils as if they were instruments of crime. David got on well with the elder Paige, who treated him now with respect, asked questions. When the meal was over, Gill invited Liz to look round the house; Mrs Paige senior joined them.

The place, square and well built between the wars, was huge round a magnificent staircase, wrought-iron banisters, with a great glass light, like a flower overhead, and a stained-glass window, pale but enormous, behind. Each room was large, beautifully light, and the pictures, mostly watercolours, tasteful without being insipid. The mother-in-law mentioned Anthony's interest in painting.

'He wanted to study it when he was younger but his father wouldn't allow it.'

'Was that the right thing?' Liz asked.

'If he'd wanted it badly enough, he'd have gone, father or no father. Daddy knew that.'

'What did you say?'

'I didn't interfere. In any case I thought Oxford was preferable.'

'And he never discussed it with you? I ask because I've got a daughter and something like this may come up. I'd like to be consulted.'

'With a daughter, perhaps, yes.' Eileen Paige was in no way put out. 'But we have a good family business. Phil's father really worked at it. Painting's just a weekend occupation. And he wouldn't have been any good, would he? Not in any real sense. He's plenty of spare time.'

'Does he regret the decision? Now?'

'I don't think so. He doesn't paint, anyhow. He has money, this house, travel. And he's good at his work.' Mrs Paige nodded towards her daughter-in-law. 'Nor would he have married Gill, if he'd been an art teacher.'

'That would be the end,' Gillian said, as they walked on in warm, sparsely but marvellously furnished rooms, on mushroom carpets, under brilliant lights, the world put into its place by wealth.

'Look at your father,' Mrs Paige said. 'And he's what they'd call a success.'

'I'd rather not,' Gill answered. Mrs Paige shrugged fiercely, walked from the room.

'Silly bastard.' Gill again, through her teeth.

The men downstairs occupied themselves with conversation; Anthony and his father sat opposite each other, David on the old man's right. They rose on the advent of the women, and Mr Paige waved his cigar.

'Where's Daddy?' Gill asked her husband.

61

'He went out.' Anthony poured drinks and as soon as all were seated, Paige senior quizzed Elizabeth about the house; his manner harried, but was intended, she guessed, as jovially friendly. He gave the impression that he had chosen the building, its décor, had modernized, and above all had paid for it. He did not say as much, but his proprietorial concern could only mean that. Wincanton came back, ran his fingers through rather greasy hair, and by his awkwardness made it clear that someone had stolen his seat. He rescued his glass, so they knew the elder Mrs Paige was the culprit. She offered to change, but he sat grumblingly down on a hard chair by his daughter. Paige continued his catechism. How did Elizabeth judge a home: comfort, convenience, a place for entertainment? She had no difficulty, claiming her homes had been decorated by chance, but in so far as it happened by choice, in arrangement of the random objects they had acquired.

'Do you mean that you've never set out with an empty room and decided, either for yourself, or with expert advice, how to fill it?' She answered easily that the thing about all art, and this was a minor branch, was the mounting of obstacles.

'So that's the way you go on, young man, is it?' Paige demanded of David.

'David's generous,' Liz answered. 'I just prefer to do it like this.'

Her husband looked Philip Paige up and down, not insolently, but as if he'd seen him for the first time.

'One should judge by the finished effect,' he said. 'You come along and tell us how Liz's rooms can be improved, and she'll listen to you.'

'He knows nothing about it,' Eileen Paige joshed.

Paige continued to lay down the law, obviously to impress Elizabeth, while Wincanton gloomed into his glass, with sighs like a horse's whinnying, plucking at the cloth of his trousers on the tightness of his knees, bored, uncomfortable, not disguising his malaise. Mrs Paige senior drank a great deal of gin, though it seemed not to affect her. Faces grew redder; conversation jerked; when at eleven David suggested it was time to leave, the company became animated, almost agitated. Wincanton stood, quoted Donne, took Eileen Paige by the arm. Father Paige strutted, making a last effort to convince the Watsons that he was worthy of acquaintance. From all this Gillian stood aside, in a disdain, shown in her mouth, in her reluctance to speak. Only Anthony, smiling, nodding, helpful with coats, seemed at home.

'What did you think of that, then?' David said in the car. 'Happy families.'

Liz did not answer, hoping her husband would confess disturbance at the people he had almost joined or wrecked. 'You made a great impression on old Paige. He'll be offering immoral suggestions to you before long.'

'Is his reputation bad, then?' she asked, languidly.

'No idea. Did you like him?'

'Not really. I wish he'd have talked about garages or whatever it is he knows about.' David licked his lips. 'Where did the young Paiges meet?'

'At Oxford, I think. Is Gill's father any good?'

'Yes, he is. Though I haven't read anything lately. I must try again.'

'Is he still writing?'

'Journalism. I don't think I've seen . . . I can't remember a novel recently.'

'But he's been good?'

'Yes. I'd say so.'

'He hadn't much to say for himself.'

She didn't answer, believing that David used this small talk with her as children practise scales, to prepare for more important occasions. They had resumed marital relations, and David had hinted that a second child might do them good, but she had set her face against that, silently, not arguing. Now, tonight, he took her arm, asked, 'Are you all right, Liz?' He'd not put it more strongly.

'Yes.'

'You seem preoccupied.'

'What about?'

When Elizabeth rang Gill Paige to thank her for the evening's entertainment, the other spoke sharply.

'Those bloody old men. They get on my tits. Phil, who's as illiterate as a beetle, talks all the time, and Rod-God, who can string a few words together, sits there blowing and farting. All to make a good impression on you. You'll get an invitation to the Paiges, one of their bun fights. Go, just for the devilment. It'll bore the bum off you, but you try it.'

'What are they good at?'

'Sod all. No, that's wrong. He runs his business well enough. He's really a smart back-street trader, but he's got good accountants, and he pokes away at them, makes them work. Can't occupy himself, though, any more than my father.'

'Is he writing anything, now?'

'He spends a fair time at his desk, types out plenty of words. He can't get on so fast; his breathing apparatus has something genuinely wrong about it, but he perseveres.'

'Is he on with a novel?'

'Ah, that's it. He gives the impression that he is. I rile him, tell him that a novel nowadays is as ephemeral as journalism. He'd like to think he was producing an undying masterpiece.'

'Is he on holiday now?'

'He's getting free board and lodging. Not that I care. He's not much of a nuisance because I keep out of his way. And he's going through it.'

'Why?'

'He's getting old.' Gill cackled. 'He's sixty-two, but you'd guess he was seventy. Tell him fifty-five if he asks you. Better not. He'd fall in love with you. You're his type. Tall and stately.'

'Was your mother like that?' Liz asked.

'No. Middle-sized, ordinary, clever, far-sighted. Everything. Not creative. That's what she said. And him. Didn't understand what in hell she meant. What's the difference between a creative and anybody else?'

'Produces works of art.'

'Thinks he does. There was more art in a flower arrangement or a meal she cooked than in his proclamations.'

'He wrote three good novels.'

'Never got to the end of one. Too bloody embarrassing. I could tell what he was writing about. He'd disguise it, but I could recognize what he was flashing, and why.'

The two arranged to meet, to go to the commercial cinema, and there Gill changed her mind at the last minute to drag her companion in to see a film set in Victorian London, lamplighters and top-hats, where girls copulated with dissolute moustachio'd men, and fell loving into each other's arms when the furniture was clear of hairy male torsos, and where Handsome Harries knifed themselves, faces in holy ecstasy as blood dripped down their genitals. Liz, uncomfortable, sickened, tried to judge the audience, but when the lights came up, and patrons shuffled for ice cream, she found she could not distinguish them from a bus load at rush hour, a half-holiday crowd in a stately home.

'What's wrong with me?' she asked Gill, and explained.

'Don't you find it amusing?'

'No.' Liz grimaced. 'Did you get David in to see this sort of . . . ?'

'Him?' Gill blew lips out in unbecoming exasperation or unbelief. 'I couldn't get him . . .' She stopped. 'It's the first time I've seen a film like that.' She pouted her innocence.

'Why did we go?'

'I wanted to. Experience. Don't you ever feel shut out?

You think I'm mad, don't you? I suppose I am, looked at like that.'

Gill talked, spewing words, even when they ate in the Koh-i-Noor, where she knew the curries were mild but beautiful. Uncomfortable, Liz tried to answer, but soon realized that was unnecessary, as her companion kept up her febrile word-torrent whether she were interrupted or not. Now and then, she apologized for saying too much, but that was mere habit, and Liz wondering watched her companion who often repeated herself, as if some compulsion rather than wish dominated her. She seemed happy enough, pleasant, laughing, excited, a man would have exulted in her company, but Elizabeth wanted her to calm down, shut up.

Her last remarks were more pointed. As she stepped smiling from Liz's car she said, 'My father's threatening to ring you up.'

'Yes?'

'I told him you wouldn't want anything to do with an old wreck like him, but he won't be said. "She's the wife of a really successful man." That's how I put it to him. "The people she meets are the people our society admires".'

'You, for instance,' Liz answered in anger.

'Don't be a bitch. I'm just warning you. Friendly. I'm your friend. Thanks for the outing. I'll go and have my bout of indigestion now.'

6

Gillian Paige telephoned before her father.

The weather had brightened; early summer showed promise. 'Would you like to see the rhododendron gardens in Lea?' Gill put pretty sentences together about the scent of azaleas in sunshine, but Liz refused, lying, setting her face against a revised date, claiming pressing duties. True, she felt guilty, invited Gill and her father round for coffee the next morning, and there John Watson made a hit with Sir Roderick as he described his time on the footplate.

David may have inherited his brains and competitive drive from his mother, but the old man had a beautiful lucidity when he talked about his own interests, and understood and anticipated the nature of Wincanton's questions. Gillian watched them moodily, snarled once about men and boyish proclivities, but Sir Roderick overrode her.

'I was responsible, you see,' John Watson said, voice slightly nasal. 'If there was an insufficient head of steam, I had to answer for it, not the fireman.'

'Did you pick the shovel up, then?' 'Shovel' sounded exotic in a southern mouth.

'More than one occasion, I can tell you. But once you were on the big expresses you had very experienced men who could judge it to a teaspoonful. It's a skilled craft, both driving and firing. Nothing to it with the diesels; your work's done for you. The machine's more efficient and so it doesn't need the coaxing. And you're more comfortable. You could get cold and wet and scorched down one side and dirty, filthy dirty.'

'You wouldn't have missed it, though?'

'I ask myself that, often enough. These new diesel-electrics, these electrics do the job better. We shouldn't retreat, should we? It's not like making something. If you manufacture tables by machine, they're different from a hand-made job. Better, perhaps, in some ways; cheaper, certainly. But I got from A to B, no more. With difficulty, sometimes. We hadn't the acceleration of the new stuff; when you slowed down for a curve, you could only get back gradually. But the idea is to provide fast, clean, efficient travel. So, oil crisis or not, I wouldn't go back any more than to a stagecoach.'

Even Gillian grew quiet, or passive, during this conversation, and when the visitors were leaving said, 'Isn't he a marvellous old man? Not in the slightest like David, though.'

Watson himself stuck his chest out.

'D'you know, Elizabeth, that's the first time I've ever spoken to a knight?'

'Is that good or bad?'

'I liked him. He's overweight. Must be a strain. And that breathing. Like a grampus.'

Wincanton phoned her his thanks, and followed with a long letter detailing a quarrel with a poet which had festered for years. Why he imagined she'd enjoy this she could not guess; why he needed to set it down at all was more obscure. It read with liveliness, seemed the work of vigorous maturity. Henry Fayne Coleman had grown a beard, 'to hide a multitude of chins', and once, in the foyer of the RAC these two rivals had been so incensed that they had found themselves grappling with the other's lapels, and had both stepped back, shocked. Wincanton made fun of himself; he'd appeared the bigger clown, grabbing the coat of the older, smaller, rotund OM. 'He's the manners of a weasel; his breath reeks; two wives have left him, but he's written half a dozen poems that will be read when everything I've written has mouldered. It's odd, isn't it, that our age will be judged in a thousand years by what this pig-eyed paranoic has put down, but it will be right. Now and then his compulsions and inadequacies, his embarrassments and rebuffs, his scores and his talents have come together in such a way that people will envy us for having seen him, never mind spoken to him. And the likes of me will stand damned because we opposed him, bawled him out, and we'll be remembered, if at all, because of that and nothing else. It's an unfair world, and as I grind my teeth I can't help rejoicing that the Creator made himself with such an ironical mind, so bent a bent.'

Liz, flattered by the confidence, decided to save the letter, but did not reply. She showed it to her father-in-law who read it without comment. Some time later in the morning he told her about a public row between two union men over the annual order for seed potatoes, and later again said, suddenly, coughing slightly with nervousness, 'Are you and our David getting on well now?'

'Why do you ask that?' Much as she liked him, she would not encourage impertinence.

'We've been talking about quarrels all day. It made me wonder.'

'I see. We're padding along.'

As he narrowed his eyes, he seemed suddenly shy, and sly and cruel, unlike the decent man.

'Was it you or him? Dissatisfied?'

'You'll do no good asking, will you now?'

His face wrinkled as if she'd struck him. His head jerked away.

'I want to see you two happy,' he said, in the end.

'Look,' she said, concentrating on him. 'Why do you question me and not David?'

He rocked his head, nursing chin and left cheek in his left hand.

'It perhaps seems the wrong thing to say, perhaps there's something amiss with me for saying it, but I like you more than I like him.'

'Why don't you like . . . ?'

'I didn't say I didn't like him. I like you more. That's what I said.'

'Thanks,' she said. 'That's nice. For me, anyway.'

'I see you're not going to tell me anything, and I don't blame you. I'm like that myself. If there's anything up with me, I'll drag myself off into a corner like a cat that's sick. Some people can blurt it all out. My next-door neighbour in Sheffield, young woman, not much older than you, well, some of the things she comes out with . . . I'd be ashamed to think about them, never mind saying them.'

He was away; he rounded off his story, inconclusive and unrevealing, and crept off, dashed down, sadder than he deserved. He did not, however, give up. She loved him, in her annoyance, as he tried again.

'We had rows, you know.' He appeared in the kitchen, where she waited for Miranda and the *au pair* back from school. 'David's mother and me.'

She opened her eyes wide, cocked her head to one side.

'About what?'

'Me, and my jobs. David and his education. She could be sharp. More like David, but he's learnt to keep his mouth shut. I think her life didn't satisfy her, that's the top and bottom. I don't say she married the wrong man, because I don't think she could have married the right.'

'That's hard,' Liz laughed.

'Ay, reckon you're correct.' He laughed with her. 'If our Jenny had lived it would have made a difference. Daughters don't mind telling their mothers off, informally, if you see what I mean.'

To have got a mention of Jennifer out of him spelt a triumph, she knew. The child had died aged eleven, suddenly with pneumonia and heart failure, the year David had decided to leave the grammar school at sixteen. Liz could imagine the house; it explained John Watson's pained reticences, those sly, wary glances at her, the hums and ha-s that twanged like noncommittal strings through his shoulders.

Yet he and Miranda grew in friendship.

At Whitsuntide the sun burnt fierce, and the old man sat in the garden, sporting a yellow panama. The enormous lawn, nearly a thousand square yards, the wide borders, the shrubberies beyond the great limes and sycamores, relics of the squire's park, overawed him. The machines in their sheds, the pond with its wide lily leaves were too large for private ownership; he had established no sort of relationship with the gardener. They spoke warily; could they have disagreed, they might have become cronies, but both retreated. Grudgingly Watson once let out to Liz: Annie would have approved of this.

Now he sat on a rustic seat, parrying the darts Miranda made in his direction. The girl lost years when she played with him. The smart miss who could read, hold her own in adult conversations, now pretended she approached a lion in his den. Sometimes she flounced smilingly to within a yard or two from the front, and stood until he made a pounce. Then she flung herself shrieking away; it was best if his curled claws just touched her. At other times she crept up in the rear, to tap his back. On the few occasions he caught her, he pretended to eat her, mouthing the cheeks and neck, while she howled with delight. The child's face glowed red with her exertions; his hat had a cheeky tilt.

'Oh, Mr Lion,' she said, 'I'll steal your meat.'

'Grrr.' Very gently.

'I'll steal your meat, and tickle your feet, and make you fall right off that seat.'

He leapt a yard, pawing the air. Her shrieks could be heard four avenues away.

'You're not tiring Grandpa, are you?' Liz asked, appearing with iced lemon juice.

'He's tiring me,' Miranda gasped. The child seemed preternaturally reasonable, so that however excited she became, the moment he said, 'I'll just read my paper, now, for a minute,' she made no objection, would go off to her own devices, or, sitting next to him would scan the news with him, commenting and questioning. 'My,' he'd say to Elizabeth, 'that child's got sense enough to vote already.'

He quarrelled with David about returning to Sheffield. His house would be unoccupied from the end of June, when he'd have it repainted and then get back, he said. David did not raise his voice.

'Look, Dad,' he said, 'it's not sensible. You're not in our way here, and if we're in yours you can lock yourself in your room. You're no trouble.'

'What about my garden?'

'If it's six foot high in weeds, and we know it isn't, what would it matter?'

'It's my home, David, my garden.'

'I realize that, but there comes a time, you know, when you can't be entirely independent.'

'That time hasn't come. Not yet, any road.'

'The doctors seem to think so.'

David never argued at length, and confessed to his wife that his father would leave them whatever was said. 'There'll be a next time. That's what worries me.' He grumbled. 'He seems happy enough here.' They watched him talking to Anna-Lise, the *au pair*, a scholarly strong blonde, who enjoyed her exchanges with him; anything she told him about Hamburg he capped with an exaggerated anecdote from Sheffield. The girl laughed all the time, but he kept his face straight so that she was never sure of him. 'You are pulling my leg,' she'd say, and his face would assume a mask of mischievous innocence. 'You mustn't think,' he'd say, very slowly, as if reluctantly forced to yield up the truth, 'just because it's South Yorkshire, nowt happens there.' 'Nowt,' she'd burble back, 'that is wrong. You mustn't teach me that.' 'Why,' he'd say in reply, 'if "nowt" were the only thing wrong in Sheffield, it'd match heaven.'

'David's right,' Liz would tell him.

'Always is. Like his mother. You're very good to me here, but I miss my home. There's no Crane Street Methodists, for one thing.'

'You don't go every Sunday here.'

'No, you're getting me into bad habits.'

'It's nothing to do with us. We'd drive you down any time you wanted to go.'

72

David spent a fortnight in the States and Canada, but telephoned regularly. His father was invited for a few words.

'It's very clear,' John Watson said, impressed. 'That's another first, for me. Talking to America.' He scratched his face. 'It's a marvel. But once you've done it, the edge has gone off it, hasn't it?' He'd look at Miranda. 'She'll think no more of it than fetching her supper from the chip shop.'

'She's never done that,' Liz countered.

'Why haven't I?'

'There's no need, really,' the grandfather urged. 'That's what your grandma used to say. But I didn't believe her.' There followed stories of surreptitious penn'orths, fritters, fish bits, rewards for piles of clean newspapers.

John Watson used the phone to some effect to start the decoration of his house as soon as the renting family were clear. Determined to return, he wished at the same time to express his love for his daughter-in-law.

'You think I'm obstinate, don't you?'

'Not really.'

'And you think I don't appreciate all that's done for me here.' He broke into a trembling version of 'Love, could I only tell thee / How dear thou art to me,' aping the big-bosomed contraltos of his youth with the set of his arms and his rolling eyes. Miranda stood by, quizzically copying him, waiting for him to notice and chase her off. 'And another thing. If I go back up there, and have to be packed off into hospital again, I don't want you traipsing up at every verse end. You've got quite enough on your hands, without that.'

When Gillian Paige looked in, as she did once weekly, he'd shout, 'Here comes the Queen of Sheba,' and she'd be compared with a Mrs Simpson or Taylor or Sidebotham who'd brightened steel-workers' terraces sixty years back.

'He's not like David at all,' Gill propounded. 'He's more like a boy with a model bus. But it's inside his head. The dinky toy's the real thing.' She opened her eyes wide, and Liz understood.

It amazed her that she could even say the name David to Gill without much terror. She'd erected a partition, but had not come within a thousand miles of fathoming her husband's state of mind. The man had been willing to give up home, with consequent legal proceedings, to lose Miranda, to jeopardize the child's chances in the world, to antagonize his father for the sake of a woman who, whatever her attractions, had a history of mental breakdown. No one but a madman, distracted by his passion, could have considered such action, and yet he'd announced it, dry as a brief outline in the boardroom. What had he felt? Had he lost all feeling? That was a possibility. He was not goaded by lust or love, merely wanted a change, and as in his work he set in motion some reorganization involving millions of pounds, hundreds of lives, by means of an arid argument, so in the same way he'd programmed the marriage computer and announced the result. But he did not run his business on mere headwork, barren reasoning; clever as he was, experienced, cunning, far-sighted, he was driven by desire, ambition, power-seeking, thrust to dominate. He was no machine, however calm he made himself out on public occasions.

Thus she did not understand.

Perhaps it had been a test. He'd sometimes told her how they set up situations to determine managerial ability. 'It's no use asking them in an interview or an examination. That's over too soon. The intelligent are up to examiners. But it's when it's actually happening on the ground, when they take a decision, and then find a week later that the premises have completely changed, that's when real ability shows. The rules alter, as they go along, and they have to keep up with them.'

That seemed equally unsatisfactory.

She could give no adequate explanation for his behaviour,

74

and, however she worried her head, the whole appeared more enigmatic in that their relationship, on his part, at least, gathered strength. Considerate, tender, sexually attracted and attractive, he was all a husband could be, this man who a month or two back had gone so far as to buy a house to live in with his mistress. Was she blind? What did she fail to see? She wondered if her suspicions now had changed her. She rubbed her tongue in violent puzzlement on her upper teeth.

Gill Paige did not raise the subject.

They'd drink coffee or shop or see a film together, but kept that weekend of crude events taboo. The variety of Gillian's behaviour during the comparatively short time the women spent in company was wide, bizarrely so. She'd be in sober tears, would smash from laughing to weeping, would be incapable of mere walking about or passing the time of day so great was the physical effect of her depression, would be racked by anxieties that could hardly be traced to contemporary events, while at other times she'd be kindly, polite, delightful, sharp and then domineering, hateful, looking to snub.

Just before John Watson returned home he came back one day from the park where he'd talked to some senior citizen who went every week to an open market, where he looked round for 'summa't to do him a bit of good'.

'I'll take you,' Liz promised.

'I can take myself, thank you. I'm capable of stepping on and off a bus, y'know.'

'I wouldn't mind going.'

'All right, then. There won't be anything there, though, you want. You don't want seconds in crockery or spare pieces of carpet.' When Liz laughed, he said, 'Perhaps Mrs Paige might like a trip with us.'

'Hello, hello.'

'What's that mean, pray?'

75

'Suggesting that you invite young married women out with you. What would they say in Crane Street?' She saw the hurt in his face, because she'd hit the truth. 'I thought you didn't like her. Who called her a painted peacock?'

'She needs looking after. She's in trouble.'

'Do you think so?' she asked.

'Oh, ay. I've talked to her.' And she had thought Gill on her best, most guarded behaviour in the old man's company. 'There's something shaky behind the façade.' He pronounced it 'fass-aid', but he spoke seriously, impressed her. 'Will you ask her to go with us?'

'Why not you?'

'You're the driver.'

On Tuesday, the next market day, the three set off. The sky, summer blue under pure white dabs of cloud, suited the new leaves on the alders by the river; people did not hurry in the sunshine; mothers did not rebuke infants for dawdling, and already a queue of men stood outside the Horse and Jockey though it was an hour from opening time. Once the market had been a crowded island, but now one road only passed it, and the stalls seemed less higgledy-piggledy, in no danger of collapsing into the gutter, but were regimented into diagonal rows with space on either side. A fair number of women walked round, they had room for pushchairs and shopping trolleys, handled the goods, questioning the proprietors, but there was no shouting, no hawking of wares, no auctions, amazing last offers. Stall-keepers were quiet people, in slacks, with their hair neat, their expression neither rapacious nor shifty; they spoke, smiled, agreed like members of a rate-paying community.

The majority of the booths offered clothes, underwear, children's garments, and neither Elizabeth nor Gill found much of interest. Gillian said that the boot-stall looked pathetic, and she meant it without pejorative overtones, with its uneasy lines of children's shoes, presumably to be tried on there and then; there was no order, and one could not tell whether the shoes were brand new or not, nor their size.

'Are these cheaper?' Gill asked. 'I've no idea what things cost.'

John explained about seconds, about how overheads compared with shops, about married women making a few pounds on the side. They were standing by a counter covered with mirrors, over- and under-printed with old-style advertisements, grey ghosts of discontinued soaps, cigars, limousines, chocolate; at the far end horse brasses, ugly bells, lumpy metal animals and cars cluttered a corner.

'Aren't they hideous?' Gill made no attempt to keep her voice down. The stall owner licked his lips.

'Better than bare walls,' Watson said.

'Did you have pictures when you were a boy?' Liz asked.

'Not many. Two photographs of aunts in fancy frames, and antlers. Upstairs framed texts, with flowers or a stretch of lake in the corner.'

'Tell me a text,' Gill said.

'In all thy ways acknowledge Him, and He shall direct thy paths. Proverbs iii 6.'

'One for me, now,' Liz laughed.

'When thou saidst: "Seek ye my face," my heart said unto Thee: "Thy face, Lord, will I seek." That's one of the psalms. I'm not sure which.'

'Shame on you.'

'The words were in letters made of rustic sticks, with bits of ivy twirling round.'

'Have you still got them?'

'No. I don't know what happened to them. Dustbin, I expect.'

'That sounds sacrilegious,' Liz said.

'You don't have texts,' Gill asked the stall-owner, hoity toity, 'do you?'

'No, lady. It's nudes, now.'

They moved on, and Watson presented each with a roll of sellotape at a knock-down price.

'Will it stick?' Gill asked him, excited.

'So hard you won't get it undone.'

They argued over the purchase of a cheap brooch on a card which he bought for Miranda.

'It's rather nice,' Liz said, pointing to the blue glass jewels. 'Will it tarnish?'

'It in't gold, you know,' the stall-keeper answered.

'These baubles give children more pleasure than anything else,' Gill said.

'How do you know that?' Watson asked, musing. 'More to be desired than gold, than much fine gold.'

'You're not the only one who can remember what it was like to be a child.'

'I'll buy you one.'

'You're sweet.'

The proprietor wrapped up Miranda's present in tissue paper, already involved as he handed back the change in another casual transaction. They cast an eye on the piles of dirty paperbacks but were charmed by the greengrocery stalls where apples and oranges lay boxed in lines and the brass pan on the spring balance shone with elbow grease.

'Men used to go round with a horse-and-cart in my day,' Watson said. 'You could buy your vegetables at the front door. The man with the loudest shout lived in our street. He wasted away to nothing.'

He insisted that they drank a cup of tea from a van. It was strong; they had all refused sugar.

'The cups are really clean,' Gill said.

'Can you taste the Lysol?' he pulled her leg.

A fat, old man, shopping bag in each hand, waddled across, greeting one of the loungers.

' 'Ow are you?'

'Awright, youth. Are yo'?'

'Ahh.'

'This is Indian tea,' Gill said, examining the brown liquid.

'Red Indian,' Watson told her.

On the way home, Liz dropped her father at the news-agent's shop where he'd get postcards he'd failed to buy on the open market. Gill invited her in, but she refused.

'I really enjoyed that,' Gill said. 'It's another world. And he's marvellous. He's nothing like David, is he? Amazing. He's so simple. No, not like that. He gets pleasure. He sees so much. You know what I mean.'

'The world in a grain of sand?'

'If you say so.' Immediately Gillian sounded huffy, dis-turbed, as if her companion had spoilt something. She wanted her own uninterrupted pronouncement, perhaps rightly. She'd been introduced to experience outside her ken, and wished to struggle into the new language necessary to make some satisfactory, explanatory comment. He betters my father. Why?

Watson sent off his cards Sheffieldwards to announce his arrival, and a week later he and Liz drove up there. She stayed for three days, to make sure he was comfortably settled. Though he'd hardly admit it, the contractors had decorated his house neatly, and the late tenants had treated his furniture with respect. The cleaning woman worked efficiently, and erupted a lava of gossip to burn out his ignorance; he answered monosyllabically, but it sufficed.

Elizabeth took him out, insisting. They visited the street where he was born, his own open market where he bought Miranda a second ring, the ground where he'd played foot-ball as a young man, and finally Crane Street Chapel. That stood gloomily enough, in red brick darkened, with steps the length of the foyer, and thin, marbled pillars. The windows, rounded at the top, seemed black, and the stone facings the colour of coal. Plaques remembered benefactors, and the scroll above the windows, Crane Street Primitive Methodist Chapel, 1882, though damp seemed needlessly flamboyant.

'What do you think, then?'

'Very good,' she said, smiling.

'Speak the truth and shame the devil.'

'A bit grim. Severe.' She risked it. 'Unfriendly.'

'It's not a picture palace,' he muttered. He narrowed his own eyes critically. 'More rain on it than sunshine? That's right. And yet, do you know I'd sooner be in there than in any other building you could name, Westminster Abbey, Buckingham Palace, St Peter's Rome? This is none other but the house of God.' He said it cheerfully.

' "A serious house on serious earth it is." '

As she toed the paving-stones her father-in-law approved, puzzled; she did not explain.

'Is this where you were married?'

'No. That was at Annie's chapel. In Chesterfield. Where her parents lived.'

'And David was christened here?'

'He was. And kicked up a fine row, I'll tell you.'

A month later, in June, she stood again, in bright weather, on that pavement after John Barrett Watson's funeral. He had died one evening in his living-room, leaving on the table an unfinished letter to her, describing how well he'd been keeping, how much he'd done that day in the garden. Presumably he'd felt tired, for he told them in his telephone calls that letter-writing bothered him, though he insisted on the practice, had made for his chair, where the cleaning woman had found him next morning. The television was switched off; the curtains were undrawn; the body showed no sign of distress; he'd been reaching for nothing, clutching at nothing. His biro lay neatly by his notepaper; the cups and plates were washed; he'd nodded off.

Now, in Crane Street, they stood for a few moments before the procession drove to the crematorium. Unimportant men, in black ties and trilby hats, shook hands, called her husband 'David'; women said they were sorry, turned to talk to each other. The muted voices were not inappropriate to the shadow of the chapel across the narrow street under the high, free blue of the sky. 'We are here to thank God for a good man,' the minister had said. 'For such men as John Watson we should meet in thanks every week for the next twenty years.' In the dark building with its varnished pews, garish organ pipes, the shiny, Sunday suits, subdued dresses, all listened, sang lustily. 'But saints are lovely in His sight; / He views His children with delight.'

David's face was pale. She could not tell what he thought. He remembered names of former neighbours, but stood apart. He showed no emotion in public, and his quietness discouraged familiarities. There, hatless on the pavement, he was one of them, but different. To his wife he had said little about his father, disappointing her. On the evening of the funeral over a drink back home, he suddenly claimed, again distantly, as if it were a matter of no importance, that he'd no belief in the afterlife. When she asked if he wished he had, he smiled.

'It never crosses my mind. Any more than a conviction, say, that I could fly.'

'What would your father have said?'

'He knew.' The question, his answer did not disturb him. 'He was very narrow in his outlook, but he'd enough commonsense to accept the inevitable.'

'Was your mother religious?'

'She went to chapel. She never expressed . . . doubt.' He smiled again at his own hesitation. Liz told him, emotionally explosive, what his father had said about Crane Street.

'I believe you.' He cracked his fingers. 'It seems little enough.'

When she broke down, he sat unmoving, opposite, waiting for her to recover. His silence spoke his love.

7

Elizabeth watched Roderick Wincanton advance along her drive.

She reminded herself of the description of Dalila approaching Samson, so bedeckt, ornate and gay, a stately ship of Tarsus, bound for the Isles of Javan or Gadier. A disclaimer: not 'female of sex', though with the bobbed, grey hair, sagging face, shapelessness of outline, that was not improbable. She could not hear him, of course. He'd be puffing, blowing, sighing. She smiled as she went towards the door, saying out loud, 'What thing of Sea or Land?'

He took her arm; she led him to a chair where he seemed loth to release her. 'My dear lady,' he wheezed, 'my dear lady,' holding her hand. This performance demonstrated his sorrow, regret, pity over John Watson's death, though he did not yet say so. It took him five minutes to steady himself into the comparative peace of heavy breathing. Nodding, gripping his handkerchief, he indicated that he would drink coffee, his face discoloured, misshapen, blotchy, baggy, deeply cut with zigzag wrinkles.

When she returned he had composed himself, mopped his head with a bright handkerchief, apologizing.

'You don't mind my inflicting myself on you, now.' Gillian had arranged it all by phone. 'That daughter of mine was only too willing to get rid of me for an hour.'

'Is she well?'

'Fit, fit. Impatient, as she always was. I don't know why I came to see her. She's restless, always has been. As a small child.'

She asked about his literary work, and when he had finished groaning about commissioned pieces and committee meetings that obstructed real writing, he described the novel he was engaged on. 'It's about growing old in a violent society.' As soon as he said this, he looked up, mouth gaping. 'Growing old. I know about it. But perhaps that is preferable to dying prematurely, like your father-in-law.' Now he spoke of Watson, how well they had got on, how lively he seemed, how controlled, definite.

'That is what I resent about old age. The lack of control. Not gross bodily functions, thank God, not yet, fundamental defects, though I've had a bit of prostate trouble. But eyes, balance, strength aren't good, and as to these bloody lungs.' He tapped his chest rudely, as one discouraging rumbustious, leashed hounds. 'Spells out the time when it'll be all beyond handling. I can get about. I can set words down, but it's a struggle. Not the fight of a craftsman and his material, rather the failure of will caused by bodily incapacity.' He looked up. 'I have always been an optimistic person, not phlegmatic or melancholy; I've had periods of depression. But even then I could remember good times, and expect them again. That's the point. Expect them again.' Pausing, seeming to sweat, he groped for his coffee, which shook in his hands. She feared for the safety of her china. He supped noisily but efficiently, returned the cup to table top. 'Now, even reason underlines fear.' Once more he spoke of Watson, his sturdy virtues, interests. Rather reluctantly she described her father-in-law's heart attacks, explaining how he hated to be dependent. 'And that's what would have happened this time.' She spoke as if instructing herself. 'He would have had to live here, or in a nursing home, waited on. It wouldn't have suited.'

Wincanton stroked his cheeks, examining perhaps the corrugations, the sprouting hair.

'Did he ever get depressed?'

'He must have done.'

'Didn't he say so?'

'He didn't complain. It's not much use when you live on

83

your own. He wouldn't have a cleaning woman until recently.'

'A remarkable man. I envy him, you know.'

'Isn't that an exaggeration?' she asked. 'When you die, you'll leave your books, and the possibility that they'll last. What did he manage? Trains on time. Influence for good, marginally, with some few individuals.'

When Wincanton had straightened his legs in front of him, he rearranged the cloth of his trousers with small plucking movements of thumb and finger, making her wait.

'Thomas Hardy, a man who had both literary and material success, in large measure, said at the end of his life that he had done all he set out to do, but that he didn't know whether it was worth doing.' The voice rolled, deep, as in a lecture hall, directed at hundreds. No wheeze, no breathlessness adulterated the quality.

'We all say foolish things when we're ill, or down.'

'That's right. And I am down, and old, and ill. And that not only makes present literary work nearly impossible, it reinterprets the past, distorts it. Let's look at both points.' She could not help thinking he enjoyed explaining his catastrophes. 'First, a writer, however pessimistic, must at least believe there is a future for his work, in so far as there is, at worst, one sympathetic reader, at best larger numbers.'

'Is that right? Suicides leave notes.'

'I mean writers. Men and women who have trained themselves, disciplined themselves to make works that they are convinced encapsulate truths about life expressed with such force or delicacy that people who have been trained equally in reading would understand and finally admire. That's very roughly expressed.' He grinned. 'It needs disclaimers and qualifications. But I think you have the drift. Since everybody, even the most illiterate, has considerable experience in the use of language, the difficulty at reasonably high levels of literary achievement is clouded. You see?' She did not, but nodded. 'You may argue that a writer needs setbacks, wrongs, tragedies, the ills the flesh is heir to, to bring out his greatest power. This may, to some extent, be so, but there must exist inside him, however faintly, a hope, that an audience will present itself on whom his words will exert effect. Let's put it no more strongly. I believe this is so, this hope, even with an author like Kafka. However desperate his state, however much his writing seems directed by his nervous instability, he wrote. That's the point, he wrote.' He suddenly seemed to see her, to redirect his attention from the hundreds of his audience. His face creased, into smiling, feminine concern. 'I don't convince you, I think.'

'Well . . . ,' she did not know whether to argue. 'Madhouses must be full of people scribbling away, and they're hopelessly insane. And what they write is worthless, which seems even worse.'

'Perhaps you're right.' He'd collapsed, sagging into his chair, at her opposition. She must stir.

'It's really interesting,' she said. 'And what about your second point?'

'Second?'

'You said your depression reinterprets the past?'

He looked at her as if she spoke Chinese. She felt pity for the abject, sluggish creature.

'You said,' she began again, leaning forward, pretty student at seminar, 'that it made it nearly impossible to write, and made you reinterpret the past. I didn't quite get that.'

He roused himself.

'Your memory's good,' he said. 'Mine's going. Gone. Yes. Now. Yes. Reinterprets. Yes. This is so. How you feel now affects how you think about what you've done. I wasn't considering my literary work. It was Gillian. I wonder how much I am responsible for the way she is now. This is something I've often considered. But not with the overpowering sense of guilt I feel at this time.'

'You can't be solely . . .'

' "Of comfort no man speak." '

' "No nor woman neither." ' She matched his Shakespeare, but he felt out in the air with his hands.

'I spoilt and neglected her, I suppose. But. You don't want my confessions, do you?' He had straightened himself out, had finished his coffee, crossed his legs and displayed his well-made suede shoes. She'd lost her moment.

'Yes.'

'Yes, what?' he asked, surprised.

'I want your confessions.'

He drew in a huge lungful of air, but reluctantly, as if through the stumps of rotting teeth. 'You know, I take it, that Gillian has had nervous trouble. Depression, acute anxiety states, debilitation. These began in adolescence. As a child she was lively, precocious, as you might expect, clever, pretty; everything her mother and I wanted. This meant, I must admit, that I spoilt her, when I was at home. At the time I was greatly occupied. I travelled in the Far East, as you know, several longish periods. I will say this for myself that I was not afraid of work. I turned down no jobs. I was in my late forties, and strong. Perhaps I went at it too hard, and that's the cause of my present,' he pursed his lips, 'fatty degeneration. That's the first thing. Secondly, on my return from Thailand I had an affair. It did not last long. I see now it was of no importance in itself, but it made a breach with my wife that was never satisfactorily healed. Of course, Ruth and I were reconciled, but . . . . I'm speaking like this to you in a way of which I don't approve. If a critic treated my novels with such black-and-white, plain-cause-and-effect examination, I'd feel rightly aggrieved, but there's some truth in it. I once wrote a line of poetry that has stuck in my head. I lifted it, I think, from James Jeans the astronomer. He was the scientist we all read at the time. "No finger moves without disturbing stars." If there's truth in that, what can the effect of my behaviour have been? Gilly would have been fifteen, sixteen at the time. I never really left home, but for the period of nearly a year, and that almost immediately after my longest oriental absence, I was irregular, and the visits were, let us say, stormy. Ruth did not allow me to forget what I was doing to her. Why should she, you may ask. I tried to shield Gillian from what was happening, but my wife did not. She made a confidante of her, blackguarding me. I might have expected it.' Now he tapped his chairarm, with slow, double handed flaps, as if in some weird code. 'The girl seemed unaffected, cheerful, doing well at school, taking part in plays, and it was not until she was in the sixth form, and I was safely gathered in, to hearth and home, that she began her, to show symptoms of her present, of the . . .' He paused, staring dully at Elizabeth, before he made a sharp, impatient movement, lifting himself from the seat, and twisting. The turn was unexpected in so heavy a man, almost like a muscular spasm, but he settled again.

'More coffee?' she asked, prettily putting a hand to the silver pot. He appeared not to hear.

'You must be bored,' he said. 'And I do not know myself whether the full account, not this half-paragraph, makes sense. But, and here we have, belatedly, my point. My present state of mind, of health, convinces me that I am wholly responsible. This cannot be right. I can apply reason, suggest dozens of other causes which moulded Gillian as she is, all equivalently weighty, but I cannot shake clear from my guilt. I guess this is why I am putting this into sentences, however badly, for you this morning, in the hope, I use that wretched word, that keyword again, that I shall exorcise my home-bred, half-baked devil. I have not spoken about this to any other person, and the fact that I am spilling it, slopping it over, to a young, attractive woman not as old as my daughter, I guess tends to surprise me. You will treat it as confidential, I know. I do not understand it myself.'

She nodded her head, held her knees together with laced hands, the model of discreet propriety. He heaved himself straighter.

'We were speaking,' he said, 'of your father-in-law. Do you think he was tempted in this way? As I was? You see, Elizabeth, I think of myself as an uxorious man, monogamous.'

'I never heard of anything.'

'Are writers more likely to commit adultery than engine drivers? Some tame, idiot sociologist must have done the research. A more bohemian society, absence from domesticity in pleasant surroundings? Ah, contiguity.'

'Railwaymen lodge away from home,' she said.

'I suppose they do. I never thought of . . .'

'He was religious. In a strict sect. That made a difference.'

'Perhaps his physical desires were not very great.'

'Or sublimated.'

He poked a finger violently into his left eye, shifting the already crooked glasses.

'You and I, madam,' he said, 'are talking like bloody fools. I beg your pardon. I am, and encouraging you to do the same. We are asking questions which neither of us has the remotest chance of answering. That is a ridiculous occupation.'

'But interesting.'

'In that while appearing to think about one's problems, one shies away from them.'

'Are you less happy,' she asked, 'than you were twenty, thirty years ago?'

'I was never happy. I have a skin short. I easily take offence. Moreover, whatever I do I can visualize ways of doing it better, and resent my shortcomings. This is not a recipe for contentment. And further, I am too interested in myself. This is a fault of my profession, perhaps even a necessity, but it leads to misjudgements. If by your question you mean: Am I settling down, easing off, giving in? The answer is that I am not. Don't make out that I'm a saint. I have compromises galore in other parts of my life, and even more hypocrisies. I'm slower. I'm the villain of my own pieces.'

This forced her to think, to pursue his hares through undergrowth of her own devising.

'You make yourself out to be wicked and hypocritical and guilt-ridden and unhappy. Surely, that's bad. Even for a writer.'

'Why do we rate tragedy above comedy? Because we must face life at its worst. Your father-in-law believed in providence, that all would be set right in some other juster world. I don't believe that. There's no evidence, and I have no faith. I don't think I even want to believe it. Nor do I have any time for rebirths. We have one shot here, and we must make of it what we can. We struggle; we die. If we're lucky we make our little mark, but even with the greatest the mark's erased in a few thousand years.'

'What about Homer?' she asked.

'The majority of people alive today have never heard of him, even the majority of European descent. To a few educated people, he's a name, coupled with vaguely remembered stories. The schools no longer teach Greek. When did you last read a translation of *The Iliad*? If we go on as we are doing, a few hundred years will make him as important as Hoccleve or Ennius.'

'Moses, then? Jesus? The Buddha?'

'I have no reason to think they'll fare better. The human animal is prone to self-deception . . . .'

' "The innocent and beautiful have no enemy but time." '

'Everything, everything.'

'Including evil?'

'That's arguable. Human qualities will last, but the matters we're concerned with are dependent on language, and lang-

89

uage decays. As English disappears, our protagonists will become mere shadow.'

'Won't the new people provide their own heroes or religions?'

'Possible. If society is literary. Literature may be as ephemeral as journalism or the television. These produce producers, men highly regarded, and front men, even more famous, but no one can remember them after a year or two's absence.' He squinnied at her. 'Of course, English may not disappear.' He sounded petulantly aggressive, perhaps because he was destroying his own ease.

She provided more coffee and he provender for argument. He had a small obsession, he said, with the machines of language, and their preserving and standardizing effect. As he talked, he seemed to forget her, so that she concluded he was outlining the thesis of some article, honing his thoughts on her for use elsewhere. She watched the face, like some unlovely, moving, half-inflated bladder, pursuing the grotesque act of conversation. Finally she intervened.

'Did you ever discuss your novels with anyone?' she asked.

'No. Not while I was writing them. I'm secretive. Or I got into the habit. George Eliot thrashed hers out with G. H. Lewes, but not I.'

'Was your wife not interested, then?'

'Yes. It was my occupation. She became used to it. I guess your husband talks less to you about his work than when you were first married. He's busier, you've other concerns, he depends less on impressing you.'

That was astute, she thought, though David had said they were not getting on well. When he'd claimed it first, she had not agreed, but had been wholly caught up in the other announcement, that he was deserting her. Since that day, she had wondered what he'd meant because the subordinate words had surprised her. Perhaps he'd thrown them at her irresponsibly, feeling he ought to have some excuse outside mere sexual attraction for ditching one woman for another. On the other hand, perhaps he had spoken the truth. They had talked, planned, shared Miranda, discussed hospitality or holidays, but it was likely that she had not shown him the admiration, devotion, give it what starry-eyed term he would, she had demonstrated in their first year or two together. For all she knew he was a great big schoolboy who needed patting on the head, praising, garlanding, presenting with prizes, and she had failed both to see and do this. Too neat. This argument was over-simplified.

The truth was she'd no idea.

And that was perhaps the crux. All married people changed, grew satisfied, or fat or didn't listen. Nobody could expect to remain what he or she was on the day they met, became engaged, went on honeymoon. They'd be lunatic to act as if it were so. She could remember how impressed she had been with David in that first year at university; she had known no one like him. His dedication, his single eye, ruthless judgement, the admiration he compelled from others, even his seniors, had set him apart. Was he less successful now? Certainly not. He was not now merely elected president by a group of students or gaining first-class honours out of clever, but oh, so limited, simple-minded college examiners, he made big money, advised governments in his spare time, ruled the lives of hundreds, thousands. Why, why, why, then had she gone askew?

Ignorance.

When she first knew him, she hardly knew him at all. Now she had lived eight years with him, had nursed him with flu, sorted out his laundry, noted his tetchy moments, his bursts of pleasure. She'd caught him out, now and again, not often, in lies, heard him, again, not frequently, boast. Without argument that was it. She'd now dotted the i's of observation; she knew him too well, left too little play for her imagination.

That ought to have led to real admiration, based on truth,

Oddly, she admitted, it had. Then she hadn't shown it? Marriage was like that, learning about the partner, then putting up with or shutting out areas she disapproved of, but at the same time dimming the praise, edging all, good or bad, nearer to that middle region that meant safety.

Elizabeth grinned as she slipped through these thoughts. This was not their first outing, but each time she managed some simpler, more elegant version, more statable. As long as she did not believe she formulated the exact truth, she enjoyed the exercise, and if offered at least an explanation for those killing sentences David had cuffed her with: 'We haven't been getting on too well, recently. Well, have we?' Her attention dipped back to Sir Roderick who was still expatiating, unaware of her mental absence.

'Of course, Ruth had the right to blame me. I left her to cope with all family matters. That's a father's failure, most fathers'.'

'And had she no advantages?' Elizabeth hoped that was the right expression.

'Yes. She met some interesting people, travelled with me to some interesting functions. I can't help feeling sorry that she did not live to share my knighthood. I should have asked her whether she wished to change her style and title.'

'More responsibility on her?'

'Hmm. I never thought of that. She would have liked it. We're a snobbish race.'

'And you?'

'Worse than most.' His cackle of dry laughter reminded her of Gill. 'But I've wasted too much of your time parading my prejudices.' He rose, and as soon as he stood his disability made itself plain. Swaying he dragged in air, he supported himself with the fingers of one hand to the table. Nevertheless he continued to express his pleasure, lavished compliments, appeared ridiculous.

She guessed that this man who could hardly take two

steps without winding himself was in this grotesque way expressing love to her. It hardly bore consideration and yet she was certain. 'My dear Elizabeth' and 'dear lady', old-fashioned courtesies dropped gently as he leaned towards her, obsequiously, as if he might bow, but for all his lightness he intended them seriously. She examined the seamed face again, the untidily long, thin hair, the scrawny neck. An old woman; he needed pearls and a twinset. And yet his hands were still beautiful, delicate, unspoilt by swollen veins, unsightly liver spots; the nails shone well-manicured and healthily pink. What did he think he looked like? Was he so used to flattery? His voice, deeply serious, cascaded on. 'I am returning to London tomorrow. There are two conferences to attend to, my editor to see, a pile of books a yard high for reading and review. But if you ever come up to town, please telephone me, and we might have lunch or dinner together, and continue this conversation. It has been stimulating. You have shaken me out of my lethargy. Merely to look at you is a joy, but added to those perceptive, snagging questions of yours, well. I have never spent so profitable a morning, not for years.'

'Your daughter is a strikingly beautiful woman.'

He seemed to have difficulty in understanding, in switching subjects. His mouth dropped slightly open; he scratched his cheek.

'Yes,' he said, in the end. 'One notices. Even where charity begins. But she is not, dear Elizabeth, your class.'

'That's a matter of personal taste, isn't it?'

'And experience. But you're probing again. I'll leave before I make an even bigger fool of myself than I am doing.'

He made his way out, in no hurry, shaking hands, touching her sleeve, slobbering over her. Flattered and repelled she watched him waddle the drive wondering if she ought to have offered to drive him back and considering his Georgian language. 'To look at you is a joy.' What next? *'The bird and leaf are fluttering breast to breast.'* She had to admit that she had been sufficiently influenced to use an old-fashioned mode herself – a strikingly beautiful woman – that cliché from the prosy magazines. Should she run after him or leave him to try his lapidary phrases on bus drivers?

She turned to her kitchen. He raised a hand to a closed door.

8

'Let's go out for lunch,' Gillian said, three days later. Elizabeth flatly refused. 'Tomorrow, then. I've just got Roddy off my back, and that calls for celebration.' Elizabeth mentioned husbands, the evening, dining out. 'I've been reading a book on this county, and I ought to see something of it.'

'We're going to America as soon as Miranda breaks up, 17 July.'

'No excuse. I'll take you out to some literary place of pilgrimage.'

'Where's that?'

'Langar.'

'Never heard of it.' She must chase the woman.

'Who wrote *The Way of All Flesh*?'

'Samuel Butler.'

'Right. Have you read it?'

'No,' Liz answered. 'I tried *Erewhon* at school and bored myself to death.'

'He hated his father,' Gillian said. 'I like that. I'm going to read it. Roddy said Butler was due for a revival, and made me cart him out to case the joint.'

'Is it worth seeing?'

'I don't know. That's just it, I don't know. There's Daddy muttering on about the hate that son had, and he hadn't the least notion that I'd push him off any church tower any day. He'd no idea. Just none.'

'Because it's not true.'

'Don't you believe it. He's . . .'

'He,' said Liz, 'is a different generation. He is, in his way, a man of consequence. Unlike most of us he's done something with his life. Perhaps he doesn't use language as we do. You think he's pompous. We've nothing to boast about.'

'Make no bloody mistake. It's nothing to do with pomposity, or pontification in the Sundays, or his sodding novels, or his jowls or his paunch. I hate him.'

'Why?'

'Because he's him.'

'What sort of answer's that, now?'

'It's nothing to do with rationality, if that's what you mean.' Gillian's eyes bulged, not beautifully. Her neck flushed. She dug her pointed nails into the palms of her hands. 'It's irrational, but I blame him for all that happened to me and my mother, and nothing's going to change it.'

'That sounds unfair.'

'Right.' Gillian looked pleased. 'So what about the trip? Help lay the ghost?'

'Whose car, then?'

They travelled in no sort of hurry in Liz's Austin through pleasant flat fields, on sunny roads, over the Fosse, towards Leicestershire.

'Have you noticed,' Gill asked, 'how many dead trees there are?' They began to count. 'Are they elms?' Neither knew. Gill, rather in her father's fashion, made mock of an educational system that left two of its graduates utterly ignorant of the names and shapes of common trees.

'A friend of mine knew the word for a lime tree in four

European languages, but couldn't recognize one though the road he drove to work on was lined with the things.'

They were enjoying the outing, the company, and with car windows open laughed out loud. Once, they had just waved at some old man wobbling on a bike, Gill put her hand on Liz's thigh, very lightly.

'Understand,' she said, and stopped. 'I shan't do anything about Daddy. You know that, don't you?'

'I'm glad.'

'This is no Greek myth.'

Now they were silent, as Liz slowed down. Fields were bright with the summer, hedges green, shadows dark blue on the verges. Gillian shuddered.

'Somebody walked over my grave.'

'Let's consult the map.' The unnecessary chore revived their spirits. They parked outside Butler's rectory, and sat in a mild stupor of admiration at the bucolic pleasures of eighteenth- or nineteenth-century life.

'I don't want to get out of the car, I'm enjoying this. But I arranged to collect the key. You won't be disappointed, will you? Promise?'

'You've seen it. You should know what it's like.'

'I was with him, and simmering. I can't remember anything. Not a thing. Oh, I can put out a few words, a name or two, but I can't see, you know, see anything. I wanted to knock my head on the wall.'

'Look, Gill,' Liz said, 'there's no need for us to do anything except turn round and go home. If it upsets you, why bother?'

'It's not the place. I want to see it with some ordinary, everyday, sensible woman with me.'

'Thanks.' Both grinned.

'I want to see what it really looks like. I don't know. I honestly don't know. And I feel I ought. I came here; we parked not a dozen yards from this spot. I got the keys, and made conversation at the door with a very pleasant woman, but I might have been drunk, or concussed. So I must see myself what it's like.'

'Why?'

'Why? He prevented me.'

'Look, I go to no end of houses, restaurants, theatres, and if I'm preoccupied or worried, or let's say, suffering from a cold, or the curse, I barely remember anything about them. I might just recognize them if I went back; I expect I would. But it's often happened, and I don't go chasing there again saying I can't remember them, I must see them properly. It depends. If I think I've missed something interesting, then I might take steps. But I'm just as likely to think the place hadn't much to recommend it or it would have impinged on me, cold or no cold.'

'I'll get the key.' Gill spoke chilly.

'I don't want you upset.'

'I shall be all right.' But she waited as if she expected some comforting reply before she left the car, crashing the door shut.

Once they were inside the churchyard, a fresh wind ruffled the long grass, tempered the sunshine. Gillian had lost her anxiety, and giggled at the moon-faced angels on the seventeenth-century gravestones, and read out epitaphs, commenting that the poets here were not altogether sure in their verses of the ultimate salvation of the souls of the corpses below. She said she liked it; it showed a proper realism, this absence of pious hopes, sentimental twaddle.

'Good Puritans,' Liz suggested.

'They did fight it out rather in this part of the world,' Still bending to the little tombs, Gill said, 'The last time we went out together, it was with John, your father-in-law.'

'Yes.'

'He's dead now. Like these. I suppose he was cremated?'

'He was.'

The trees swished, the grasses rioted in the wind. The church above them stood stolid, yellow green in the sun.

'Butler's father restored it,' Gill said.

'Some use for fathers, then.'

'I don't deny it. Why should I?' She seemed delighted with herself as she let them in, humming to herself, jinking the keys.

The nave was both larger and lighter than Elizabeth expected, so that it was like stepping out into another sort of open air, or a modern barn of a sports hall, high, and sunny, all air. The absence of old pews emphasized the spaciousness, and bright contemporary chairs were dwarfed leaving great areas of deserted floor to be walked on, better, run on, clapped round. Even a cursory examination spoilt the first impact, for plaster was cracked, paint peeling. At ground level all was well, swept and garnished, but the high places were left to God, and his bright day outlined the extravagance of ambition, the mouldering, untouchable reaches, the reverses in ecclesiastical wealth.

The two women walked about.

They passed the ugly raised vault of the Howes blocking the end of the south aisle, then the Sunday-school corner, with its bookcase, its small coloured chairs, its oblongs of daubed pictures, stick-legged angels, leaping, cock-eyed animals, a jamjar of faded flowers. They examined the box of the organ in the south-west corner, and when Liz had lifted off the lid above the manuals, Gillian began work on the hand pump. Stops were pulled out and a chord of C major laid down. It pealed, frightening both by its strong life. Gillian swore, and the wind ran mournfully out. Liz restored the status quo.

'Here endeth,' Liz, remembering Larkin. Gillian stared down at her feet, frowning, caught out in some childish sacrilege.

'I've got the transept keys,' she said, louder than necessary.

The technical word surprised, restored sanity; two highly educated ladies were walking sedately round an Anglican church.

To the south first with its magnificence of monument. There the marble flowed into convolutions, and the notables lay stony-faced to heaven, features less beautiful than clothes.

'I wonder if they actually looked like that,' Liz wanted to know. 'Or did the sculptor just guess.'

'Worked from a portrait. They obviously employed somebody out of the ordinary. Thomas, Lord Scroop of Masham. Philadelphia, his wife.'

'That was the name of one of the traitors in *Henry the Fifth*. With Richard Earl of Cambridge and Thomas Grey, Knight of Northumberland.'

'So it was. Only that would be nearly two hundred years before this. Same family. Perhaps.' She walked to the base of the monument and tapped the kneeling mannikin. 'This little brute,' she said, 'left three illegitimate children. One of them married a Howe. That's how they got into the act. The Glorious First of June brigade.' She pointed at a wall tablet, lifted a cover. 'Nothing about Valley Forge, though.'

Elizabeth's eyebrows rose.

'Helped us lose America. That's a good thing. I approve, I suppose,' Gillian said, hoity-toity. 'It's dusty here. Let's try the other side.' Gillian made much of her stint at turnkey, shaking the doors, ushering Elizabeth through as if she were a party of schoolgirls.

Across in the north transept they stood by another tomb, Chaworths this time, in a place of damp and muddy dust. Rain had recently darkened one corner, a flat, wooden cupboard had twisted with moisture. Gillian walked crossly round this place, as if its decay were to be blamed on her. She peered at the lower end of the monuments, by the east wall, and called her companion over to see the carved shoes, the intricate petticoats, hidden under the long frock.

'Real craftsmen.'

'If they don't soon make this place waterproof, they'll be losing the lot.'

'The upkeep must be enormous,' Gill said. 'It's like servicing a little palace.'

They stood, soberly enough, but not in depression.

'Have you seen it now?' Liz asked her companion.

'Seen it?'

'When you came in with your father it made no impression. Or so you said. Was it worth coming back?'

'Change and decay,' Gill said. 'Yes, it was. It's worth seeing for what it is. Last time I thought, if that's the word, about Butler and his Pontifex and his hatred. That seemed the point. It loomed. I couldn't bear Roddy's blowing, and I wanted you to be in it with me, part of the anger. But you're not.' Gillian ran blood-bright nails through the fine darkness of her hair, and breathed deeply. When she spoke again, her voice was flat, complaining. 'It spoils it, makes the whole thing ridiculous, when you try to put it into words. It was elemental before, wild. But that was me. Now you and I have visited an imposing church gradually decaying in a small village, the birthplace of moderately important men. That's worth something. I'm glad I've seen that, and had my mind changed for me.'

She locked the transept door.

Once more they looked round the spaces of the church. Elizabeth read a note which made it clear that this organ had not been installed in Butler's time. She passed the information on.

'He was quite a musician, wasn't he?' Gill said. 'Thought there was no other composer but Handel, as I remember.'

'Some man.'

The church, the trees, the sky were bright now, polished, compared with the rough drabness of the church, the damp, the silent decay, the ephemeral signs of modern use.

'That was good,' Liz said, as they strolled back.

'Do you think so? I'm glad.' Pathetic inquiry. 'Look at the plums there.' Green fruit hung in abundance high over the road. 'I can forget about this now. I couldn't before. Do things obsess you? Now I feel quite calm. I could go home and write a schoolgirl's essay on "A Visit to Langar".'

'You won't, though.'

'I'll do the equivalent. Tell Tony about it.'

'He'll enjoy that, will he?'

'He won't understand what's going on. When I came here with Rod he spent the whole of dinner expounding to Tony. And I sat there, shaking, just shuddering with rage. I could hear what he said, but it didn't register. And Tony tried to stop the flow, by asking me a question or two. I just choked on the answers. I couldn't talk. Literally.'

'So when you go back, with a blow by blow account . . . ?'

'He'll ask me if that isn't the place I went to with Daddy. And why have I been again.'

'And?' Elizabeth enjoyed this slow walk, talk on a village street.

'I shall tell him I took you, and then he'll be happy as a lark for the next twenty minutes telling me what a marvel you are.' Gill laughed, took her companion's arm. When she handed over the keys she spoke with real pleasure to the woman at the door, stayed to make conversation, showed herself a sociable being, unhurried on a long summer's day.

They dawdled over a pub sandwich, but were back by three to begin housewifely duties. Twice again Gillian mentioned the visit with her father, but cheerfully, prosaically. When they parted Gill's thanks seemed effusive, almost schoolgirlish, as if this striking woman's appearance hid some uncertain adolescent. But Liz, proud of herself, could not help liking her companion the more for that.

9

The American holiday was successful beyond expectation.

Miranda, wide-eyed, made friends in the hotel with an American family from the West Coast on a similar jaunt to their own. Their father, a medico, absented himself, and the two girls, both older than Miranda, made a pet of her. Clothes and accent constantly caught her wonder.

'If you look at their faces,' the child told her mother, 'they're just like anybody else, but their dresses, and their hair. And when they begin to talk.' She imitated their accents, their argumentative tones, their refusal to be impressed by any of their mother's marvellous proposals.

The young Stettins were noisy, lively, clever, but overawed by the solemnity of Miranda's pronouncements. They insisted that the two families took their outings together, and then waited, Liz thought, for the English girl to cap everything, to provide them and their friends with topics of endless conversation. They spent some exhausting hours together in the Egyptian rooms at the Metropolitan Museum where Miranda was alternately breathless and then furiously inquisitorial at the riches. The children vied at pointing out this treasure or that out-of-the-way bit of preserved domestic debris, moved like manic detectives, only barely muted their excitement, but in the taxi on the way to the hotel Elizabeth, half-drugged with fatigue, could hear her child instructing the colonials.

'It is superb,' she said. 'My daddy said it's worth coming to New York just to see that, and I think he's right.' Liz wondered why the child put on this know-all air. Perhaps for the same reason that when she'd played in the garden with her grandfather she'd aped the infantile. It was her kind of art. And David, alleged connoisseur of museums, seemed equally a work of the child's imagination. The careful voice continued, its English accent precious as ancient Greek, beautiful as hieroglyphs, to the audience. 'But in our little castle at home, there is something I like better.' They clamoured for enlightenment. 'It's a mummified cat.'

'There were plenty up there today.'

'Yes. But I really know this one. It's like your cat at home.'

'We don't have a cat.' Libby, the younger, sounded disgruntled.

'I wouldn't say,' Miranda continued undeterred, 'that it knew me, because that's impossible, but I know it. Nobody else bothers with it. I can think it's mine.'

'But it isn't.' Cynthia, the elder.

'I know that. I said I could think it was mine. It seems not part of the exhibition, because there's not much. Today was overwhelming. My little cat would get lost in there. She might be frightened.'

'My, my.' Miriam Stettin shook her head, eyes sparkling with admiration.

'I'd like to see your cat,' Libby said, grudging the admission.

'And it's in a castle.' Cynthia.

'It might like to see you,' Miranda conceded.

'Can it?' Libby asked. 'See?'

'Not really.'

The Stettins shook their heads with delight at the little sage.

Elizabeth described her daughter's performance to David, who laughed, and said that the showing-off was good, educational, a sign she was not wasting her time.

'You mean she's overcome with it all, and has to try to equal it with a performance of her own?'

'Something like that, I expect.'

'She does it well.'

'I know. Miriam Stettin talks of nothing else. Won'erful.' He imitated badly, grimacing. Just for that moment he reminded her of his father, who, when this trip had first been discussed, talked of Li'l Ol' Noo Yark, a phrase from the age of films, she presumed. 'But she's a right little jingoist, really.'

The American family had visited Hollywood, and were willing to describe. The names fell: Beverly Hills, Bel Air, Sunset Boulevard, but in spite of their fluency they lacked the seriousness of mien that made Miranda so matchless a talker. They had seen the hand and foot prints of the movie stars, the fantastic houses, but the cinema meant little to them. In England there still existed people who had visited the pictures three and four times a week, and had seen to it that their children and grandchildren were versed in the great names.

One day in Central Park, the children had been dashing about in the brilliancy of the weather, Elizabeth heard the Americans pile wonder after wonder in their description of Disneyland.

'Real whole streets,' they said. 'You can walk down. And the fire brigade and the band.'

'And the frontier, the Wild West.'

'It's real.'

'I should like to see that,' Miranda admitted.

'Get your Mom to take you across. The covered wagons. Dad said you could taste the dust.'

Liz was glad that Cynthia and Libby had found a topic to silence Miranda. She didn't listen any more than she did to Miriam, who complained that Gaby worked too hard to do justice to his family. Occasional murmurs, a sentence of praise now and again for the appearance or intelligence of the children were sufficient to keep the monologue running. Now Cynthia described the flame at the Kennedy memorial;

they had stood solemnly there; these bright energetic children of European Jewry were full Americans, aware of destiny, it seemed, part of the great ruling nation. Suddenly Liz, day-dreaming, sun-drenched, became aware that Miranda was talking, taking over.

'And there it was in the wall, a kind of circle. Not very big.' Miranda distanced her hands, perhaps eighteen inches apart, concentrating as if an error by a millimetre counted. The Stettins watched. Miriam had stopped her harangue, and her facial expression exactly mirrored that of her children. They watched as if between those small, slightly waver-ing hands some miracle would manifest itself. They would have liked, Liz thought, to have halted the games, the pedestrian performances, the hot day's humdrum and to have gathered a crowd to hear this prodigy, this oral Mozart.

'And do you know what it said on it. In old-fashioned letters. Eighteenth century, I imagine. "Entrance to the Vault".'

'Could you take it out?'

'I couldn't. No. But a builder or a mason could. And though it was so small, men could have wriggled through, and passed the coffin, and laid it with the rest.'

The others breathed admiration.

Liz realized, she must have been sun-struck, that the child was describing the Howe tomb in Langar church. Miranda had not been there, but was reconstructing the description from her mother's account, and the subsequent discussion with David on how much of the wall would be removed for an interment.

'And in there is the general who lost to George Washing-ton when he could have beaten him because his soldiers were starving.' She raised an inquiring eye to her mother.

'Valley Forge.'

The Americans smiled. Perhaps they had heard of it. Like Stamford Bridge or Marston Moor, not in the top rank of battles, but . . . Liz, succumbing to the magic of her daughter's words, smiled again, patting her hair.

'I wish I had seen that,' Libby said.

It must have been the English voice that worked the miracle, because the Stettin children were not short of material, nor of words. They talked on, and Miranda took it all in, but when she began she spoke as one having authority.

'We have never been to Europe,' Mrs Stettin confided. 'Would you believe that?' She laid a hand on Liz's arm, a great toucher. 'We shall have to make it now.'

The Watsons ended their stay with a trip to Washington, and the parting between the children was tearful. That so much emotion could be generated by a few meetings, meals, expeditions, chats staggered comprehension, but during the three days in the capital Miranda walked sadly, tight-lipped in bereavement.

'What's wrong with her ladyship?' David asked.

'She's missing the Stettins.'

'Is that it?'

'I'm sure. They made a celebrity of her. She liked it.'

'They were nothing out of the ordinary, were they?'

'Who is?' she asked.

'Who is? What are you talking about?'

'Conversation with you is not improved when you don't listen to a word that's said.'

'I'm sorry.'

That was the truth, but he did not understand the wrench. In New York, a new city, large, friendless, unsafe it was said, she and Miranda had found themselves at home. Both doubtless exaggerated; the ambience encouraged such instability of response, but she missed those two fair-haired, crisply dressed children reporting at their room each morning in controlled, rising excitement to escort Miranda to breakfast. If she, an adult, felt like this, what would Miranda suffer? The child observed and remembered what she saw, but the fact that the President was not in Washington meant nothing beside the absence of Cynthia and Libby. Liz knew she was alive.

They returned to England, slept long. Miranda painfully wrote to her friends in San Diego, but then followed silence. The child watched the letterbox for a day or two, but resigned herself to her preparations for the next holiday, in Cornwall. On the morning she and Liz set out, cards, fancifully decorated with huge stamps and postmarks arrived. The Stettins were swimming every day; their mother said they'd soon be fishes; the doctor would attend a conference in Birmingham later in the year. Was this near? Miranda said nothing, but carefully stored the mementos in the fascia board of the brand new Volvo Estate David had bought for family outings, though he was not accompanying them on this jaunt. Liz, afraid of the responsibility, drove down in two stages, enjoying herself not at all. She noticed that Miranda consulted the cards at least once on the journey, and carried them into the hotel at the stopover.

'You're pleased to hear from your friends, aren't you?'

'Yes. They were especially nice.'

'They were. That's right. I liked them.'

'Do you know that they had never seen any snow in their whole lives?'

'Poor deprived beings.'

'I told them you didn't like it, but they wouldn't believe me.'

'Did you tell them how cold it was, and how it congealed into nasty ice, and how filthy it got?'

'No. I didn't remember that. I described what it was like when the snowflakes fell.'

Cornwall was good, in a hot wholesome August, and again they made friends, but distantly, casually, not concentrating on one group. Miranda mentioned she had visited the States, but here she concentrated on beach games, dashes into the sea, walks inland, being photographed. She directed her whole energy into building sand castles, or threading in between sunbathers with ice cream, or chasing a beach ball. She acted her age, as if the American trip had demanded a maturity of which she now divested herself. Brown, freckled, she wore herself out, slept long in spite of the heat.

David rang just before dinner each night, was consideration itself, hurtled down overnight to spend one weekend with them. He looked pale and tired, so that his wife chided.

'Why don't you take a week off?'

'I'm into bad habits.'

'What does that mean?'

'This is my best time for thinking.'

'When your family's away?'

'Nothing to do with that. When we're slightly slack and there's not much day-to-day demand.'

'Do the others feel the same?'

'I don't know. We all follow different lines.'

'And you're the brains of the outfit?'

'You could say so.'

Though he lightened his tone, she could believe him. Now he considered what the group had done, and what was possible. She imagined him in his office, or his study, making notes on scraps, rewriting, expanding, meticulously filing, defying chance. Commerce he treated as a form of higher mathematics, but when she said as much, suddenly as they were swinging Miranda on the street in St Austell, he argued.

'No, it isn't really. But I'll give you this. It does a firm good to have somebody about who can deal with it in that way. One, two, three, swoosh. You're getting heavy. Otherwise contingency bogs one down. Ideas coming up like that can be useful. But that's not the real secret of making big money these days. One needs a team outside with contacts which'll work twenty hours out of twenty-four when it's necessary, and a team at home that's brilliant at improvising inside limits so that contracts can be managed that don't look possible with our plant, and on time. Again? I haven't the breath. And your mother's wrists are limp. What do you say, you young monkey? Your grandfather sometimes said "wrisses"? And bread crusses? Come on, then. One, two, three, hup she rises. Of course, a group like ours has a huge foundation of steady work, done year in, year out. But you never know. Some new invention might replace the lot. Not ever so likely, not without our knowing. We're the ones who'll get an option on the new development, and we'll bring it out in our time to suit ourselves. I tell you this. If the politicians decided tomorrow that it's to be nothing but nuclear power stations, we shouldn't be the losers. They won't. They're frightened of the pollution wing and the coal lobby. But we're ready for them if they all go raving mad.'

'Why should they go mad, daddy?'

'Good question.'

'It's like mummy's poem. "If parson lost his senses and people came to theirs." '

David demanded a recitation; the child had it by heart, though she'd heard it only two days previously.

Both these performances lifted Liz.

David had brought down further postcards from the Stettins, and Miranda spent her own cash on return missives from the beachside booths. Usually she bought views of the sea, boats, churches, but the one comic aberration she regarded as specially apposite. It depicted an enormous woman leaning over a fence, her posterior a monstrously inflated balloon. Two small boys share the dialogue. 'My dad says the Americans have the biggest bomb.' 'Your Ma must run 'em pretty close.'

'It's about America,' Miranda said, sensing some lack of approval.

'It's not really suitable, is it?' Liz nosed.

'Why not?'

'It's rather vulgar. It's a pun on the words "bomb" and "bum".'

'I knew that. That's why I liked it.'

'Blame school,' David said afterwards. Miranda delighted still, had tucked the card away for personal perusal. She'd conform, but her parents were not quite certain whether they were being put to the test.

That evening when the child was in bed, the Watsons sat in one of the lounges over a drink. A serious game of bridge went quietly on in a corner; three ladies exchanged courtesies over gin; two newly married couples soberly drank in preparation for a joint foray elsewhere. Decorum ruled at eight-thirty.

'Have you heard anything of Gill Paige?' Liz, pleased with herself that she could ask the question.

'Not a word.' Unruffled.

'Where are they now?'

'Weren't they going to Brittany for a week or so? Tony had rather a lot on.'

'So they'll be back?'

'You tell me.' David sounded waspish. 'You were suddenly great friends of theirs.'

'I've not heard a word since we went to New York. But, then, I've hardly been at home.'

'She'd get in touch,' he said, 'if that's what she wanted. But that's like her. All over you one minute, and the next doesn't want to know you.'

Liz rounding her mouth registered a comedian's irony. He, understanding, lifted his glass, toyed with rather than drank from it.

'Yes, I know,' he said in the end, and putting down his whisky yawned. 'Not very generous on my part? When I think back to that time.' He stopped at the euphemism, scratched at the table top. 'I must have been off my head. Now I can no more understand it than . . . I've told you. I was like somebody about to jump from the top of a sky-scraper. Or try my hand in the fire.'

'It was what you wanted to do.'

'That's the worry. I wanted it. It seemed necessary, power-fully so.'

'Were you under stress at work?' she asked.

'Not really. I couldn't blame that.'

'She is a very attractive woman. Physically.'

'I agree. But not a touch on you, Liz.' He did not look at her, played no games.

'Different.' She might get it out of him.

'Well, yes.' He fiddled again with his drink. 'I also knew there was some history of mental instability. Not the whole story by any means. But again, I thought I could deal with it, that I could provide the circumstances to set the trouble right. That's what's so frightening. Not that she was what she was, but that I thought I could manage.'

'You mustn't have been very satisfied at home?' she questioned, gently enough.

'It wasn't the seven-year itch.' David twisted his lips. 'Home life wasn't very exciting. I mean, you did all I could expect of you. With Miranda. As a back-up for me, work-wise, you were perfect, I'd say. But I felt guilty about you.'

'Why?'

'I thought you hadn't enough to occupy yourself. Properly. You'd Mirry. And the house and garden and your film societies, but I guessed that in your opinion it didn't add up to much. You'd been trained for an intellectual occupation.'

'Not really. And even if that were so I ought to have been able to apply myself to, oh, learning Greek, or something. And if I'd stayed at teaching that's not really very demanding, intellectually.'

'But you might have felt that you were preparing the next generation. That's something. My job's not cerebral. Not basically. I'm solving no problems in the way one does in science. I'm just organizing ways round and through. Won't do next time, never mind the next millionth. But it's well paid, and highly regarded socially. So I'm satisfied. There'll never be a Watson's Law. And when I leave Waterhouse, Cliff, it'll be as though I had never been. That doesn't bother me, either. But I didn't like the idea of your playing the little woman with the duster. I thought you resented it. You did, didn't you?

'Yes. Sometimes.'

A subdued roar from the bridge table interrupted them, so that David looked up, startled. They were far enough off from the other guests not to be overheard, and presumably David often talked in public places without giving secrets away. It was the unprivate look of this room, perhaps, which had led to these confidences. At home, where a misdirected remark could lead to hysteria or violence, one did not begin a conference except out of desperation. Here in a large, well-lighted bar, shared with other guests about their holiday occupations, one could start on dangerous subjects, knowing the limitations, the necessity of keeping a straight face, a restrained voice. Only the Gill Paiges, unstable, indisciplined, would scream or scratch in this place. The fervour of the bridge table died; a fresh hand was dealt, picked up, examined with decorum.

The interruption had stopped David, caused him to reconsider. Now he was smiling at her, leaning backwards in his chair, massaging his lower ribs. She'd have to renew contact.

'I can't see,' she began, 'why all this would make you decide to leave me.'

'No, it wouldn't. No. But a striking woman suddenly set her cap at me. And I fell for it.'

'She couldn't have been the first?'

'No. Suppose not. But I fell for it. The bits and pieces must have been right. I crashed. Like a simple Primitive Methodist.'

'Why do you say that?'

'Upbringing. All repression. Thou shalt not. And when that framework gives, my God, there's trouble.'

'You'd lost the framework?'

'Oh, sure, sure. Long enough ago, I'd have said. But I kept the trappings. Must have.' David rose, picked up his glass, waved a finger at hers. 'Sup up.'

She allowed him to replenish it, but as soon as he returned she spoke, sharply.

'It's a funny thing. We sit here discussing these matters. We've had a good day. I'm having a marvellous holiday. But we're not trying to understand what happened, are we? If I know you, you were a lot clearer in your mind about what was going on than you make out now.'

'Why do you say that?'

'I've known you nearly ten years and if you think I believe you'd ditch your wife and daughter, antagonize your father without knowing what you were about, then you've got it sadly wrong.'

'That's how it was. Exactly.'

'No.'

'I can't force you to believe me. I'm not a rational human being all the time. And I tell you that I knew what I wanted, to abscond with Gill. It lasted, intensely, for about a fortnight.'

'Long enough to get a house.'

'Investment in property is not bad, even these days. A bachelor pad.'

'You'd been considering that, before, then?'

'No. It's a complicated story.'

'I imagine so.'

'Are you looking for a quarrel?' He looked severe, formidable; she could expect a rough ride.

'No. Not really. I just don't believe your explanations, that's all.'

'There were three nice little town houses going cheap. Small. Built in the garden of one of those Victorian mansions. Quick sale. Thirty-five thousand each. Bob Cheviot offered me one. I said yes. I thought I could either let it, or if my dad got awkward, instal him there. Only twenty minutes drive away. Five minutes from the hospital. So I bought it. Before I had any thoughts of Gill, or living there myself.'

'You buy a house, for thirty-five thousand pounds, and never once mention it to me?'

'That's right. I wasn't sure you'd approve. I had to take out a little mortgage.'

'It doesn't,' she said, 'sound like you.'

'What does that mean?'

'I've never, to the best of my recollection, ever as much as questioned one of your business deals. I don't know enough about it, for one thing, and second you're obviously very successful. So why expect opposition from me?'

'I didn't,' he said, 'quite trust you. There was nothing exactly wrong, but I had a feeling that things weren't exactly right either. I was like those fellows in Shakespeare who didn't know why they felt sad.' God bless 'O' level. 'But I didn't want to chance my arm, trust my luck. I've told you I felt guilty about you. And I'd wished my dad on to you just when I'd got really busy, and had to be away a lot more than usual. You had to cope with him. I thought you might take the opportunity to go for me, with this house as pretext. It may seem unlikely now.'

'I don't remember it like that, certainly.'

'I may have got it round my neck. But that's how it was. I didn't feel right towards you. Guilty. Of messing you about. Or leaving you to clear up.'

'You weren't tired, tiring of me?'

'It was nothing like as positive as that. You'd not put a foot wrong, and I didn't feel I was doing too well. That I didn't like. So when Gill wiggled her eyelashes at me, I wasn't my guarded, usual self.' She did not answer his triviality, merely looked down at the fingers touching the stem and base of her glass. 'You don't believe a word of this, do you?'

'No,' she answered too promptly.

'It's no use, then, trying to convince you. We'd better leave it.'

'Um.'

'I'm sorry, Liz. I wish to God this hadn't happened, and that I had been less of a bloody fool. Let's not spoil the holiday.'

'Shall I be able to trust you again? That's what worries me. Suppose you caught somebody out at work in blatant lies, could you be confident about . . . about, well, believing him?'

'Depends on the man and the circumstances. Yes, if I thought he was any good. Everybody tells lies. Besides, I did the opposite. I opened my big mouth, and let the nasty truth fall out.'

'What you did was worse.'

'Yes, you could say so.'

'I don't think you realize what you've done. You came out with your little joking sentences. "I wasn't my usual self", and the rest. The way I feel I shall never be my usual self again. For these last weeks I've pottered around, I've kept my mouth tight shut, tried not to think, practised being polite, hoping I'll get over what's happened.'

He watched now, determined to sit it out. She locked herself into the silence. The young married couples thanked the barman and left, earning not one glance from the bridge table. In the end, he spoke.

'Can you go on practising politeness?' he asked.

'Every time I look at Miranda I think, "He was willing to desert her".'

'I hadn't realized, Liz, that it had hit you so hard. I'm sorry.'

'Hit me hard.' She burnt his words softly on the air. Her quietly savage intonation angered him. He flushed; his eyebrows met, buckled.

'It's quite common for parents to split up now. Quite common. And the children, by and large, get over it.'

'Do they?'

'I'm not good at being blackmailed,' he said.

'When we started this conversation,' she answered, 'I felt pleasantly tired, much at ease. Now, I don't care if I don't see you for the next six months. I could strangle somebody.'

'Me, for preference?'

'It's no joke.'

'May I remind you,' he said, 'that you began this subject? Though I can't say I'm sorry you did. It's best to be frank, occasionally. I hadn't cottoned on that you were so badly affected.' Great, increasing chasms yawned between the sentences. He swilled his whisky away. 'Can I get you another drink?' She shook her head; a tear brimmed, hung, fell. 'We'll leave it, then. I know what I've done.' He paused. 'Tell you one thing. I'd sooner you blew your top than bottle it all up.'

'It's not something that I can scream my head off once and that's the end.'

'You mean it's a matter of divorce?'

'I don't know that, either.'

'No,' he said. 'Nor do I. But it may be.'

'You can't blackmail me, either,' she snapped.

'Well, that's spoilt a good day.'

'You've spoilt a good few.'

Though they slept in the same room, in twin beds placed together, he made no move towards her sexually. She slept badly, guessed he was awake, but lay still, warm and uncomfortable. He spent Sunday morning with them on the beach, took them to lunch, delighting Miranda, and drove off soberly.

'I wish he wasn't going,' the child said.

'We'll send him a card to tell him. "Wish you were here." '

10

In the sharp brightness of early September Roderick Wincanton asked if he might call on Elizabeth, explaining that his daughter had left him to fill in time while she and Tony had a luxury weekend in Derbyshire with the senior Paiges.

'They didn't invite you?' she asked mischievously when he arrived.

'They did not. Though they knew I can't go back to my place until next week.'

'Are you cooking for yourself?'

'Salads. Cold meats. Shop-sugared pies.'

'Poor man.'

He seemed, in fact, cheerful, breathing easily. Well into a novel, he was collecting his critical essays, was pleased with what he found.

'I was up, and at work at eight this morning. That's two and a half hours solid. Their house is ideal. It's large enough for me to walk about in when I'm on my own, and quiet enough to allow real effort.'

He entertained her with his stories of literary figures, and then, on inquisition, how he first became interested in Thailand. His brother, who now lived in Hong Kong had worked as a prisoner on the Japanese railway. The two had visited the country, Malaya, Burma, Thailand, one to look again, the other to make a book. The result was remarkably unexpected. Rod suddenly found himself unconcerned with the history of cruelty, but topsy-turvy with excitement about scenery, small faces in a small population: Joseph, squinting down his nose, said nothing, made his way back to his bank, his wife, his considerable fortune. Roderick pointed a finger at her. 'One of these days I shall write the other one, the hellish railway line. I know how it affected Joe. But it's wrong, morally. I can't make play out of their horror. Not yet.'

'It wouldn't be play.'

'Yes. As I write it, it would. Even now, nearly forty years on. Joe's best friend just died on him. I knew him slightly. Bout of dysentery one night, no worse than the rest. Next morning keeled over and died.'

'Of what?'

'They didn't hold post-mortems. Presumably some weakness. Heart, perhaps, Unless he'd been sitting on some serious illness, saying nothing. Death dropped on them, then. No drugs. No care. Like Greek tragedy. We can hold death at arm's length, today. Even old wrecks like me. God.' He sighed. 'Joe's younger than I am, and fitter, so perhaps I'll never write it. I couldn't bear his reading it.'

'Does he know what you're planning?'

'He's no idea. For an intelligent man, he's no conception of books, or their making. He needs comfort. Literature's like whisky, to be taken in moderation.'

'Is that good or bad?'

'It wouldn't make much of a living for me, now, would it? And even less of a name.'

'Though you admire your brother?' she asked.

'He's single-minded. He's quietly made a lot of money, and I guess that isn't done without taking risks. But he says little. He'd work his way through his time in Japanese prison camps without complaining. He'd not look for trouble, but if it came, he'd put up with it.'

'He didn't like your Thai book, then?'

'Not like? That's too strong. It would seem exaggerated to

him. He's lived in the East most of his adult life. What would surprise me would be humdrum to him. It's this habit of catching a reader unawares that makes a travel book, don't you think?'

'People need to be taken out of themselves, yes.'

'He wrote, "Dolly," his wife, "likes your book, is very taken with it in fact. I wish I could please her so much." '

'That's sad,' Liz said.

'Not it. She knows which side her bread's buttered. It's his backhanded way of complimenting me. I was pleased the book came out as it did. Blossoms and twitterings.'

'That's unfair.'

Elizabeth explained, hesitating at first, why she found the writing so satisfactory. Under the picturesque, his words had forced her to grope for the humanity shared with his orientals. 'It was as if you'd made me question the real basis of human life. It wasn't just temple bells and flowers. I hate that sort of book. It wasn't quaint. I won't say you made me feel Siamese, you didn't. Or but for an accident of birth, you know. I don't quite understand what you did to me, but it seemed important, crucial. Rather like philosophy. I read it, and it made me question why I was here, what I was doing with my life. Beyond the problems the writer set out to expound. And it wasn't religion, the Buddhists and their beliefs. They're surprising, I suppose, but no more so to me than Baptists. You made me tell myself, "Here is a place; here are people occupying it. You also live somewhere. Now why? What's it all about?" That's not right, perhaps, and certainly I don't express myself very well. David didn't see it at all like that. He thought it interestingly described a country he'd once visited. But to me there was a second book behind the first. I found myself written there. Or I saw a burning bush in the desert. No, that's wrong. I'm exaggerating now. But it isn't just a travel book. I was very enthusiastic, I must say, am still. I think in some ways it was you the novelist who did the writing. It had something about it that sprang from the imagination.' She smiled, 'I don't usually gush. I'm sorry. You'll think I'm very naive.' She, half-consciously, had exaggerated, over-stressed, because for some reason, beyond her, she felt compelled to praise, to over-praise this man to his face, to confront him, to cultivate his desert.

'My dear lady,' he said.

He looked ridiculous now, his flushed face held askew and high, his pudgy, beautiful hands on the arms of his chair. He breathed easily, without rasping: himself an idol, reverencing his own achievement.

'I do not deserve your praise. And yet you so exactly delineate what I set out to accomplish.' He shook his head; his eyes were wet; his finger nails, pinkly oval, touched his cheeks. 'No one else has come so near the heart of the book.'

She was a hypocrite, but she felt elation over her deceit, if that's what this performance was. Perhaps she spoke more truthfully than she knew. He shook his head with pleasure.

'My dear lady.' The words wheezed from some distant era, before he was born, some Jamesian strand, some Chekhovian cave. 'I will make a confession.'

The man would spoil any bloody thing. Go on, blabbermouth, blubber-belly. 'Oh, dear.'

She asked him to stay to lunch, and he postponed the secret. Now he talked of three years on and off he had spent in Siam, Cambodia, French Indo-China for his newspaper. The trip with his brother to the prisoners' railway had formed a small interlude in this lengthy stay, but had geared him to writing a book. That it was the wrong book surprised him, but he had written, and that was good enough.

He congratulated her on the cheese soufflé, ate heartily, drank a half-glass of hock, refused a second course. Insisting on helping clear the table, washing the dishes, he said, profuse in thanks, that he would tell her what he had in mind, and then go. Flattered, she listened.

'What you have said this morning has encouraged me to try something out. I put it dully, like that, for good reason. I'm superstitious and I don't want to make too big a claim, as yet. I imagine too, that it surprised you that I, a compulsive writer, am not yet immune to flattery.' He laughed at his own ironical pronunciation of the word. 'But for these last few months I have wanted to write an adventure story. Another surprise for you, eh? You imagine that such a category occupies a rather low place in my hierarchy. As I get older, I am troubled that my audience is so limited. I would like to write so that young people, intelligent children, would read with pleasure. You've encouraged me to make a start.'

She bit back a sarcastic question, sat straighter.

'It will be old-fashioned, of course,' he said.

'Oh? Why is that?'

'The modern thriller seems to concentrate on packed, authentic detail. One learns what it's like to be a cypher clerk, or a police woman, or minor diplomat or frontier guard. At least that's what it seems. I say that because I imagine that with the best writers of the genre they make up a good deal of this apparently authentic detail. Anyhow, the interest seems to centre on that, rather than on the plot, which is complicated and shallow, and to concentrate after that on the reactions of the characters to their dilemmas, or ennuis, or crises, which are never of a major order. Spying is as boring, as painstaking, as laborious as cartography or coal-heaving. As you put it, Buddhists are no more interesting than Baptists. I admire the men who write thus, but I do not want to copy them. I want the broader strokes, the cloak and dagger, the last word on the scaffold, the heart broken in the cause of duty.' He laughed out loud. 'Fine, rubbishy melodrama it sounds, eh? But what if it can achieve what you say my travel book managed? Have behind it this second, serious nimbus for those who can see it. That would be something.'

'Yes,' she said.

'My field of fiction deals with the family, those knots of disagreement, of the effect on the small group of social pressures, politics, finances, deaths of kings, but mostly of the disturbance and distortions inside the home. I have written two such novels, half-a-dozen short stories, a play. It's a subtle and rewarding subject, but . . .'

'Yes?' she said.

'It's a subject of infinite possibilities, I am convinced, but it lacks the grand gestures. I don't say, you notice, the most important. But I feel that shattering public love, a death by firing squad or guillotine, the scaling of mountains, with appropriate speeches tempt me. For once only, perhaps. Then I'll creep back to my important intimacies.'

'Will it be set out East?'

'Perhaps, though it won't start there. I see my hero shouldering his way along Oxford Street.'

'Will he be like you?'

He levelled his eyes towards hers, and remained still, in rebuke.

'I'm broken-winded, lame, old.'

'In his ways? His thinking?'

'I shall provide the words for actions and his talk. In so far, I shall be like him.'

Now he spoke coldly, rejecting her, seeing through her frippery.

'When will you start? Today?'

'I might put down a note, an outline.'

'That's good,' she said. He buttoned his coat.

'There is an accepted framework for such a book. I shall aim no higher than writing a tale that conforms and is workmanlike. If it contains more, that will be provided unconsciously, even against the run of the pattern inside the genre. It will be what they call a bonus.' He seemed to be dismissing her, making her aware that her flippancy had been condemned, out of hand, reduced to cliché.

'Can't you aim too low?' she asked.

'We can all do that.'

He indicated that he must leave, and she showed him to the door. She watched his slow progress down the path, the flying of the coat tails of his mackintosh contrasting with the slow roll, the carefully planted sponge-thick footsteps. His hair blew thinly; his hands in pockets held down the leaping coat.

Elizabeth felt shame. The old fraud had proved himself more lively than she was. When he put words on paper, he meant them in seriousness, knew whether or not he joked, watched himself for flaws, false echoes. Ugh, she made too much of it. He'd waddle home for a nap.

A day or two later Gill Paige phoned, dashed round.

'You've had the old blunderbuss, I hear. What did he want? Don't tell me. You encouraged him. And to do what? To be the new Rider Haggard.' Gillian jerked her head, Punch-and-Judy fashion, at the question and answer.

'He was rather impressive, I thought.'

'He's a windbag.'

'Is he?' Liz asked. 'That wasn't quite how I saw him.'

'I hate his ugly, fat guts.'

They sat down. Gillian, bronze from her holiday, gleamed almost golden while she remained immobile. Only the scratching on the thighs of blood-red nails betrayed agitation.

'Is he still with you?' Liz again.

'Unfortunately.'

'Has he started his new book?'

'He ought to finish his old one instead of strutting about. He's a mountebank. Oh, I know you don't think so.'

'Anybody who writes one good poem, one good novel is marvellously out of the ordinary.'

Gill kicked her legs about, but settled to narrow her eyes.

'He's cruel,' she said.

'I hadn't noticed.'

'He used to beat both my mother and me.'

'I'd no idea,' Liz said.

'I throw it in his face now. When he's gasping for breath, I say, "That's for hitting my mother." You think that's no way to behave. I laugh.'

Gillian recalled their home in London when she was fifteen, just before he spent two years out East, and wrote the book on the Thais. 'He was in poor shape. He had been for years. He'd had a rough war, been a Chindit in Burma.' Liz wondered why he'd omitted this in his account to her. 'He'd published his first book just in 1939, and it disappeared. He'd written a second and third when he married my mother, who worked at his publisher's, and he was doing nicely, money-wise, as a journalist. I was born, and he saw to it we went short of cash. My mother had to keep his house polished, but we lived on mince and bread and jam while he dined out on expenses. And there was always another woman. He was attractive, I suppose. All my friends said so. I hated him. Does this upset you?'

'No,' Liz said.

'It should.'

'Why?'

'Because it kills me.' Gill's face stretched taut, ugly as metal. 'About this time, he got his paper to send him to Cambodia and Thailand because he'd ballsed his life up with a woman called Maire Laban. She was the same sort of bastard that he was and could get back at him. I knew nothing of this. He wasn't home much, and there was I at my Latin and Greek at day-school. My mother used to cry sometimes, and her temper was uncertain, but I was a nuisance, a precocious know-all brat and I said what I thought. This evening I was going with a young man called Jeremy Stout to a concert. A quartet from the Academy was playing locally, in a church. I'd dressed myself up, and King Lud had just come in, looked me over. He'd had a drink or two, or so I guess now. He sniffed my perfume and creased his face, and asked me what event I was gracing. I told him.

' "They're playing the first Rasoumovsky quartet," my mother said. She was pleased to make any sort of contact with him, even when he was treating her like shit.

' "Which you know well," he said sarcastically. She shook her head. I can see her now, humble, saying "No" without speaking. "Which you know well," he repeated very loud.

' "No, Roderick," she said. "You know I don't."

' "Is there any whisky in this poorhouse?" he asked. She fetched it, went back for his little cut-glass jug of water.

' "What do you get out of this?" he asked me, while he waited.

' "I like music."

' "And chocolate éclairs?"

' "Yes," I said, "what's wrong with that?"

' "If you don't know, no explanation of mine will do any good."

' "If," I said, "you're implying that cream cakes equal Beethoven in value . . ."

' "Value?" he said. "Ah, value. You'll know about that."

' "Yes," I said, "Beethoven is a great representative of the human spirit." I was just beginning in the debating society, and I used to lift phrases from my favourite sixth-form orators. "As you'll agree."

' "With what do I agree?" He made a face and looked impatiently at the door. He cracked his thumbnail unpleasantly on his teeth. "Don't tell me. Don't bloody well tell me. I have enough to put up with when the old cow's at her homilies without your starting."

'I didn't say anything, but then my mother came in, with his jug, and just before she put it down on the table she tripped and a jet, spurt of water, not much, hit him. He wore a very beautiful claret-coloured waistcoat. I remember it because the rest of his clothes were so untidy. It made a dark stain. He jumped up and howled, like a dog. It wasn't human. She just stood there; she was a tall woman, holding the jug. He grabbed it, snatched it out of her hand, and hurled it at the wall. It smashed a picture, a big aquatint of a church by a river; the glass splintered, and fell in spikes, and the paper ripped. And then he swore at her. I'd never heard such filthy language. She drew herself up.

' "There's Gillian here," she said. It must have taken her some courage. He walked across and swung at her, caught her smash across the face with the flat of his hand. She was squealing, but she still stood up to him, with her hair frizzing out of place and a red mark on her cheek. She looked awful, and she swayed about, but she didn't move from her spot. I thought he'd go for her again, but all he did was lunge past her and gave her a sort of shoulder charge, absolutely deliberate, that knocked her over. Then he didn't leave the room, turned back, sat himself down, and opened a newspaper. It was insulting. My mother crawled up, she was crying out loud, sobbing, and crept from the room. When the door shut he looked me over, politely, as if nothing had happened.

' "Hadn't you better get off to your concert?" he asked. I couldn't speak. My throat was full, and my chest. I couldn't answer. "I asked you a question," he said. I tried to say something and burst into tears. He crumpled his *Times* up and brought it down on the floor between his feet, so violently it tore. "Christ," he said. "Don't I pick 'em?" I can't remember getting out of the room. I had to wait a quarter of an hour at the bus stop for Jeremy, I was so early.'

'What about your mother?'

'She'd slink in with a dustpan and brush to clear the mess. Quite likely he'd kick her as she was on her knees.'

'Have you told this story to anybody else?' Liz demanded.

'I give a public, bloody recital of it, every Friday.'

'Have you?'

'No. Not even to Tony. He'd forbid him in the house.'

'You were glad when he went off to Indio-China or whatever.'

'Except he kept us on the bread-line. But, yes. She missed him. He was the best thing that ever happened to her. In spite of. She was like you, she admired his work. In my view he was fifty years out of date when he started, and no talent, either. I've tried to read what he's seriously written, but it's a fancy, ornamented account of his own hang-ups, no more, no less. He could put it into smooth sentences. Mandarin prose. But it was like him, awkward, crippled.'

'Isn't that why it has some merit? This counterpointing of his style with his pain or his shame?' That sounded superior and silly.

'Counterpoint? Counterfuckingpoint? You talk like him. Smooth-arsed, butter-tongued lies to cover his dirty women and his splashing money on anybody but us.'

'He was cruel, I don't deny. And you're probably right to hate him. But it's the fact that he was so unpleasant, and knew it, that adds iron to his books. He was honest with himself.'

'That sod's never been honest, anyhow. He didn't write down that he thrashed his wife, did he? Nor admit that when he came back he bullied me into a breakdown while I was trying for Oxford? All you got were his thin-cut versions of holy soul between thick slices of monumental prose.'

Liz laughed, delighted.

'What in hell's so funny?' Gill, sour as vomit.

'Your sandwich. Starve and stodge. It's not fair, but I like it. I'm sorry.'

'You've never been nagged bare by someone who hates you, who liked nothing better than to have me grovelling in tears, when he'd proved to his pompous satisfaction how ignorant I was. God, I lacked any confidence, anyway, without his ministrations.'

'But you got into Oxford.'

'And I'm what I am now, raving at you, swallowing down tablets by the handful, stealing your brave-boy husband, because of what he did to me. He mutilated. I know you think that's exaggeration, or bad form, but it's the truth, the sane, sodden, bastard truth.'

Gillian did not shout; she delivered her sentences in a fast, soft monotone, like a dictation exercise. She had no expression because she concentrated on the core of her sentences; embellishment would have burnt off, an inefficient heat-shield.

Liz was afraid.

'He's not like that now?' she ventured.

'He doesn't get the chance. But he hasn't changed. I know you think this is my illness speaking.' Gill broke off. 'That's enough of him. He's not worth the breath. Where's David?'

'In London today.'

'When I look at him I wonder what sort of father Miranda finds him.'

'They get on well.'

'How old is she?'

'Seven.'

'The sun shines out of his arse still.' Gill looked up. 'You don't mind my language, do you?'

'No.'

'I envy you. Did you quarrel at home? Your father?'

'I remember,' Liz said, 'hating him at one time, but it all passed over.'

'They're dead, aren't they?'

Liz outlined the circumstances; her mother's heart attacks, her father's stroke; their deaths within six months of each other, neither sixty.

'You've not inherited their weaknesses, have you? Constitutionally? You say he was a clergyman. I hate bloody parsons.'

'You do say the right thing, don't you?'

'Are you picking a quarrel?'

'I don't much mind,' Liz said. 'You can be as rough-tongued as you will, but if I am only politely critical, I'm quarrelling.' She hoped her trembling did not show.

'You don't like me.'

'I don't understand you, that's certain.'

Gill's face fell, into a comical, sullen pout.

'I wish you liked me, because I'm getting worse. I have to snap at people, snarl at them, swear. I don't want to. Perhaps I'm vicious, but I came here this afternoon to grouse, to say what a fool Rod was with his adventure story, and have you agree with me, while we both sipped cups of tea. And you see. I die. I flare up, and injure myself, and I die, and you hate me, you, one of the people I want to admire me and like me. I die.'

'That's not dying.'

'I know.'

'Why do you use the word?' Liz asked.

'Perhaps I wish I could.'

They sauntered out to meet Miranda from school. The child, eager with life, spoke her delight that they were walking home in the brightness.

'Don't you like the car, then?'

'No. We go back the wrong way.'

'What's wrong about it?'

'I miss the ghost tree.'

She promised to show them, hugged her secret, laughing at their ignorance. 'I tell you one thing,' Miranda said. 'The branches are above the leaves.'

'It sounds more like a riddle than a tree.'

'You wait. You'll see.'

'I'm sure it's worth waiting for.'

When they reached the old, municipal cemetery, the child climbed, then sprawled across, the stone wall, calling on them to look.

'There.'

The women took to tiptoes.

In the middle of a graveyard the tree hunched, ugly as sin. Out of its top, above its weeping leaves, whited branches crisped, bent and bare, grey like glove fingers, crooked where the wood had writhed into sharp angles.

'What it is?' Liz asked.

'Is it a beech?'

'It's a Count Dracula tree, because the earth's full of bodies.' "Harriet, beloved wife of James Martin, died February 4th, 1911, aged 56. Also their daughter Constance Mary, died March 15th, 1912, aged 31. Peace after pain."

'Where's father?' Liz asked, pointing. 'Can't be still alive.'

'They're lucky.'

'It's good, though, isn't it?' Miranda excited.

'Unusual, I'll grant you.'

'Thomas Tompkin Christian,' Miranda called.

'Well read,' Gill praised. 'That Gothic script's hard.'

'That tree's crawling up out of itself, like a skeleton oozing out of its skin.'

'Ugh,' Gill said, and lifted Miranda down.

'It's worth it, isn't it? To see.'

'Not every day,' Gill said. 'Surely?'

'Every day,' the child insisted.

They made their way back, and as Mirry hurried into the house, Gillian, refusing to trespass further, congratulated the mother.

'Isn't she imaginative?'

'They all are at that age till school knocks it out of them.'

'I wouldn't have noticed that tree, and now I can't forget what she said about it, crawling up out of itself. It's so exactly right.'

'She put on a show for you. She likes to impress. Especially really smart ladies. Not old fuds like me.'

Gillian bent to her car; the glossy photographer would have had a field-day.

'Hope I wasn't too boring.'

'The most interesting conversation I've had for months.'

'That's worse. I'd be grateful if you said nothing to David.'

'It wouldn't cross my mind.'

Gill pouted, ducked in, drove off. Miranda, emerging again, commented on the beauty of Mrs Paige's clothes, but said there was a button nearly pulled loose. 'She kept tugging it. Didn't you see? It spoilt it. You could have sewn it on for her if she'd asked, couldn't you? If she's no good?'

'I expect she didn't want to lose it.'

'She's the most beautiful lady I know.'

Liz, shooing her charge indoors, considered jealousy.

II

The next morning Anthony Paige drew up by Elizabeth, who was shopping.

'Have you had coffee yet?'

He drove her round and parked not a hundred yards from the city centre. 'Belongs to a friend of mine. Can usually get in here, and if not, there are other places.'

'Lucky man.'

He pulled a face. As they walked to the Plumtree she reported Miranda's compliment.

'I'll pass it on,' he said. 'Fear not. She loves praise. Runs in the family.'

'Has father-in-law gone back?'

'Oh, he doesn't stay. She shows him the door. Anway, he only comes up to see you.' Both laughed. 'It's true. He doesn't even bother to deny it when she goads him. Just claims you get him to work. He's writing two novels at once now, and all on your account.'

'I'm flattered.'

'He'll be good at this adventure thing. He's not all Stevenson. He'll match Greene and Golding and Fowles.'

'Do you read all these people?'

'Yes. I did English at Oxford.'

'I'm sorry.'

'The old fellow's got something. He has. Steel inside all the softness. Of course, he's ill now. But he can still grind it out. Gill won't admit it, or say a word in his favour.'

'I know that,' Liz said. 'She also blames her own troubles on him.'

'Does she, now? Is that what she told you?'

'Haven't you heard it before, then?'

'Not really. She dislikes him. Male chauvinist. And he's mean. But, no. Not.'

'She had a breakdown before she went up to Oxford because of him,' Liz hazarded.

'Had she? She'd recovered pretty thoroughly when I first got to know her. She was having an affair with a big OUDS man. Ditched him for a politician. Round to me when he didn't suit. By that time we'd finished there.'

'Didn't she work, then?'

'Oh, yes. Got a second. Some alpha papers. She's clever enough to enjoy that sort of graft.'

'Then, why . . .?'

'Does she give you this guff about her father ruining her life?' Anthony's face wrinkled into mischief. He had ordered, as they sat at a black oak table, black Italian strong coffee with demerara sugar; the waitress, naming his name, had collaborated. 'Because she thought that's what you'd like to hear. Now don't get me wrong. I'm not telling you she's healthy. She isn't. But she manhandles her misery. Shapes it. Manipulates it. You're a literary person, interested in her father. So.' He produced a spotless, ironed square of handkerchief, shook it loose, then blew his nose on it with surprising violence. 'If it were fiddles you were interested in, then she'd be driven mad by Heifetz's perfection or by being forced to practise ten hours a day in the coal cellar.'

'You're saying,' Liz spoke slowly, 'that your wife is a liar.'

'Exactly.' He laughed, patting the arm of the waitress who had reappeared with surprising speed. 'Cream now? Sugar?'

Liz directed him. 'She suits you. I might have been the *bête noire*.'

'You don't take her seriously?'

'I do, that.' He grinned; the corners of his eyes wrinkled into deep spokes. 'I came and asked your help, if you'll remember. She was driving me berserk. But she likes performances, and given a new face, she'll tailor her illness to fit, if that's the metaphor I want. Perhaps it's millinery I'm after.'

'So that tale about your doctor advising a friend to confide in . . .?'

'True as I'm here.' He licked his finger, and drew it across his well-shaven throat. 'But it's the theatricals, the new productions which do her good.'

'Did they?'

'As *my* old father says, "They did an' all".' Again a vulpine grin on the sharp features denied the perfection of white teeth, the marvellous suit, the expensively styled hair. 'You worked wonders, for which I am duly grateful.'

'But it's all over now?'

'Who says so?'

'You implied it. She needs a new audience.'

'You underrate her, Elizabeth. She's by no means exhausted your potential yet.'

Liz watched him, the glossy ad executive, the TV stereotype, the middle-aged schoolboy afraid of, and living on, his father, and decided she'd never seen him before.

'She gave your husband, shall we say . . . a matinée?' He nodded as if he'd suddenly worked out for himself the confirmation of a deeply puzzling answer. His guest did not exist for some moments, until he tapped his saucer with his little-finger nail. 'He closed the theatre down. Didn't he just?' This morning as he'd spoken, he'd lost the southern standard, fallen back on the local, accent, phraseology; she wondered if it were deliberate. 'It disturbed her. He's a cold customer. So far and no further. That's that.' He rubbed elegant hands. 'She is very taken with your daughter. Says what a marvellous child she is.'

'Aren't you interested in a family?'

'That's difficult. I'd like it. My mother and father would. And I'm supposed to treat the old man's slightest word as law.' He waved an ironical finger. 'But it is tricky. I'm not sure about Gill. I think sometimes she might. But, then, I think she's not fit to care for a child, to have the responsibility.'

'You'd help, wouldn't you? And you could hire assistance. Like us.'

'What troubles me is how she'd feel. At some times she'd convince herself that the youngster had been run over, killed, would die inside a week. This might be fantasy, but she would not see it so. So even if I, or the *au pair* or nanny had the kid under strict surveillance, she'd crucify herself in her imagination. And that wouldn't be fair to her, or the child. Bad luck.' He shrugged.

'Isn't it possible the added responsibility would cure her?'

'Do you believe that?'

'I don't know her well enough.'

'If we start a family it'll be her decision, not mine.'

'And you're satisfied to deprive yourself in this way?'

'I'd like children. Yes. But not on these terms.'

'Doesn't this,' Liz asked, hesitating, hedging, afraid of this dapper man, 'upset the balance of the relationship? Sorry if I sound like a textbook.'

'Upset? Yes. But isn't that what relationship's about? To be able to put up with discord or disagreement. I suspect we're a bit of a joke to you. I don't want to be rude, and I may be wrong, but I'm a clown in your book, a puppet in a posh suit, and she's a bloody foul-mouthed lunatic. She's unhinged; she drives me cracked; one of these days I'll break her jaw for her, but I tell you this: I wouldn't be married to any other woman.'

Elizabeth blushed, but soon she reassured herself that now he spoke to convince himself, not her, and felt better.

'That's good,' she said at length.

'In a way it is. I don't know how long it'll last. We may get into such a tangle that we split. She may dump me. I know she nearly went off with David. I only learnt that last week. Odd, isn't it? I can easily imagine myself having enough of her. But not just now. Not now. This is a proper marriage, and I'll keep it that way as long as I can.' He touched his hair. 'Sorry,' he said. 'Quite a speech.' He played with the creases in his trousers. 'You don't think like that, do you?'

'I wouldn't say so, certainly.'

'That's rotten.' His eyes, she noticed, brightened with tears. 'Has he knocked all compassion out of you?'

'He? David, you mean?' Coldly.

'Yes. I do. The machine-minder. That's what we call him. The man with the oil can.'

'I don't understand that.'

'He's a marvellous operator, don't misunderstand me, but he works it all out. On a graph. On a computer. He knows what's possible, to a fraction, and that's what he'll do. That's why he married you, isn't it?'

'Go on.' She did not like this; Tony showed his wife's vice.

'You're beautiful. You dress well. You keep his house, raise his family, shield him from what he doesn't want to do. You talk to his colleagues, and choose the right pictures to hang on his walls. You're self-confident. You don't go running to him. And if you did, he wouldn't know what to do. Or, rather, he would. Back away, slither off, and concentrate on putting the next little nut or bolt on the firm's product.'

'I didn't realize you disliked him so much,' Liz said.

'Oh, I like him. Admire him. He's a marvel, one in a million, absolutely outstanding, but such excellence isn't achieved without losses. You're one of them. Perhaps I'm talking out of my key, because it's next door to impossible to sum people up, but when I first went about seriously with Gilly, I knew she was, let's say, unsteady. Just how bad I didn't know; perhaps it was as well. But I wanted to look after her, thought I could, knew she needed me. That's how I felt. Young. Foolish. What you like. I could help her to be something that I wasn't.'

'Such as what?'

'I didn't know.'

'Do you know now?'

'Not really.'

'That must be a disappointment then.' She sweetened her voice.

'You've never had your chance,' he continued. 'You're the little lady at home, to be photographed in the sun-lounge, with the antique furniture.'

'What makes you think that's so unsuitable?'

'Because of the restricted opportunities. You've never written verse or journalism or appeared in a play. Perhaps you wouldn't have been much good. But you could have tried. You could have run a school or taken to politics.'

'In what ways are these superior to what I do now?'

'You'd be yourself. You'd do these yourself. You wouldn't be hubby's stay-at-home.'

She watched him for a moment, collected her handbag.

'I shall be second-rate at whatever I do,' she said.

'I don't believe that.'

'You hardly know me sufficiently well to lay the law down.'

'Now I've annoyed you.'

Again she waited, rather prim-lipped, as if to deliver judgement.

'No. You just let your tongue run away with you.' She rose.

'Yes.' Subdued, he apologized.

They parted outside in the sunshine; she had noticed that he had not paid his bill like the rest, merely lifted a finger to the waitress, who had moved towards the cashdesk. His face seemed paler, in the street, with a saddened smile, as if he'd blotted his copybook, and regretted it. She thanked him, but he remained rueful, incapable of bearing the sunshine.

'Is she getting better?' Liz asked, shaken by his wan appearance.

'We hope so. I don't know. If her father died now, and that's very likely the state he's in, she'd blame herself for it.'

'What can you do about it?'

'Keep on keeping on.'

He raised a hand, gloved now, and made for his car, not to be questioned further. As soon as his back was turned, she saw him again in stereotype, with broad shoulders, good clothes, a confident walk.

She gave David an edited account of the meeting, but he snapped.

'I'd have as little to do with that man as I could.'

'What does that mean?'

'He's as cracked as she is, and not honest.' He stroked his chin.

'Well, come on. Don't leave me in suspense.'

'I've said as much as needs saying.'

'He knows about you and Gill.'

'That's very likely.' Untouched. 'Do you fancy a few days in Scotland?' He showed her the schedule of engagements for the next six weeks. She would be expected to give two dinner parties and attend three, one really cut-glass, with younger royalty present. Tony Paige spoke right; she ran to David's beck and call. She tried to raise indignation, but could not; the life suited her. She would not even demand a bribe, new clothes, gadgets, trinkets. She enjoyed herself. With quiet élan, she filled in her diary.

'We're in limbo,' David said, at length, arrangements made.

'Where did you find that word?'

'It's true, isn't it? We're neither here nor there.'

'Laodicean,' she prompted, ironically. He frowned his ignorance pleasantly. 'Lukewarm. Your Methodists surely preached that.'

'Why are you so pleased with yourself this evening?'

'I've earned it. But go on. We're in limbo.'

'It worries me.' He tried to give the appearance, and looked younger, his legs stretched out, crossed at the ankles. As he bit his lip, he flapped his soft-covered diary at his knee. 'We aren't getting on well.' The diary bent harder. 'We're not, are we? I wouldn't say,' rugged smile, 'that we're getting on badly, but. But. That's the word. And I keep thinking to myself that I ought to say something. Before things get worse. If we let things drift, go by default, before we know where we are we'll . . . You see what I mean.'

'I thought we'd agreed to go steady.'

'We've done that long enough.'

'Go on, then. I'm waiting.'

He stood, jerked her from her chair, bundled her up high. Surprised, breathless she did not struggle, or speak.

'Do you surrender?' He staggered about the room with her, like a caber-tossing athlete. She did not reply. 'Surrender,' he shouted.

'If you like. If that's what you want.'

He let her slide down, swiftly, her skirt spread into disarray. She shook her head.

'Horseplay doesn't suit you,' she said. She spoke with the cold certainty she had used when she'd told Paige he'd talked too much. As then, she did not now feel powerfully, intend hurt, merely wished to test her power. 'And last time you spoke of our getting on badly, you followed it with an announcement that you were about to leave me.'

'You're not going to forgive me for that, I see.'

'I do my best.'

'That's not how it feels.'

Elizabeth settled herself into a chair, allowing time to compose herself. Mildly excited by the brief lift, she looked seriously at her husband.

'I say,' she began, 'very little to you on these matters. We've been married eight years, and I'm not sure, though I've tried to find out in an amateur way, how we should feel about it. Sex is goodish, isn't it? Or perhaps it isn't. Anyhow, it suits me. We agree about bringing Miranda up, and you do your bit there, though I . . . No, that's not fair. Now, what else can we, ought we to, look for? I do my best for you socially. You've never complained. You've not even made suggestions. So I take it I'm performing satisfactorily. I don't feel altogether, oh, compensated in some ways, but I knew what I was letting myself in for.'

'Do you want another child?'

'Not particularly.'

'I dislike this fastidious tone you adopt. I'm trying to do something for you. I owe you a great deal, and I want to let you know, but, my God, you're making it hard. We're not the couple who got married, you know, Liz. Not by a long chalk. We've lost something on the way.' He stopped between each sentence as if inviting her to comment. 'Without much gain, either.' Now he waited, fingers clasped, eyes greyly on hers, solemnly.

'I don't know how to answer that,' she said.

'Isn't that as good as a confession that there's something sadly wrong?'

'Perhaps. Perhaps not.' She watched the spurt of anger twist his mouth. He tried her out as he tested an applicant, but she would not accept the convention. Thumping a fist into a palm, he spoke.

'If you're not going to talk, you're not, I suppose.'

He stood, but did not turn.

'Haven't you got anything to say? To offer?' The last burst out like a cough.

'Since this Gill business, talk has only worsened matters. If I tried to argue I'd lose my temper and scream or rave at you. And don't say it would relieve pressure. I'd feel worse. I'd resent it. I'd blame you. So I keep quietly in the background.'

'That's why I'm, I'm disturbed. You never used to be like that.'

'I had no reason to mistrust you.'

'I was mad, Liz. I've admitted it. And apologized, grovelled. I'll do so again. I just cannot understand now what I was about. There's no excuse. I temporarily lost my marbles.'

'Do it once, do it again.' His vulgarity riled.

'I see that. Or at least, I see why you say so. But it's not likely. She's unusual. I was caught out. And exotic; I was utterly flattered.'

'Your daughter says she's the most beautiful lady she knows.'

His face puckered, into a pout of grief, disbelief, dyspepsia.

'She's tinsel, pinchbeck, Liz.'

'Those are good words. But they don't help me. Or comfort me. I don't even know if I mind. But I can tell you this, if you keep on nagging me, and probing, and poking, I shall burst into tears, and you'll have me knocking my head on the wall. I hate it. I wish your father were still alive.'

'Why do you say that?'

'Because you were a human being then. You were somebody's son.'

'And I'm not now?'

'I don't know who cares. Whether you do, or if I'm just sore because you dumped me. I don't know how to feel now, not properly. Any minute, I shall scream, because that's all I can manage, because words are too much, and I don't want you to put your hands on me. Why don't you leave me alone?'

'If I do, things will get worse, Liz. If we can't exchange a word, we're lost. Sometimes I think we are now.'

'Let's get lost.'

'Liz, we're not old. You're not thirty yet. We're young people. Is it that you resent what I'm doing to you, preventing you from being?'

She could not answer that easily, had heard it all before.

'No, it is not. You're outstanding. I'm not. I'm mediocre at everything.'

'But you'd prefer to do your own thing, however feebly.'

'I would not. I like the position as your wife. I'll do that as well as I'll do anything. And the pay is good, compared with teaching or journalism. No, David, set your mind at rest on that score. I'm not eating my heart out to be a barrister or in politics or even the WI. But what you don't see is that you've done something so horrible that it finished me. As if I'd been run over, and crippled. I don't like to say this. I don't want to make a fuss, but that's exactly how it seems.' He leaned forward. 'No, let me finish. You don't see it, I know. You've been honest with me, and now you admit you were wrong or mad. But that doesn't alter a thing. You finished me off, so that the only thing I can do is to hang around and wait to find out whether my neck's broken and wonder if I'll ever be capable of feeling anything again. I've told you this before. You don't believe it. I loved you more than you me. Or in a different way. That's all. That's what your dad called the long and short of it.'

'I'm sorry.'

'That's why I want you to leave me alone. I'm a casualty.'

'It would be wrong to leave it there, Liz.' How deeply he spoke, in what sincerity, his eyes hooded, in shame, his right hand hovering. 'If we do, we'll never recover.'

'Perhaps that's so. Perhaps I never shall.'

'Is that what you want?' he asked, voice suddenly feral.

'No. It's what I can't help.'

'You think this is the way to punish me?'

'No.'

'Or get your own back?'

She did not speak, muddy, frigid with misery. The one effort of explanation had debilitated her, so that all she could manage was to stare at his chairleg, highly polished mahogany on an asymmetrical carpet flower, bright yellow, among russets, tawny and blood-red, and listen to an attenuated voice, her own, reiterate: 'As if I'd been run over. As if . . .'

'Forgive me, Liz. Let's start again.'

That was not her husband, the man she wanted; that was some atavism to the Primitive Methodists' penitent's form, all turning the other cheek, seeking salvation under the shadow of the Cross. She could not think clearly, but she did not want this. If she could have wept all would have been healed, he would have pulled her to him, but her chest, her throat, her face set, congealed against tears. She sat rock-stiff, but then, rousing herself, put her hand on his knee. His hand closed large on hers, and she did not shrink. They sat like this for some minutes, unwilling, awkward, uncouthly relieved.

'It's the Fair next Thursday,' she said, at length.

'When are we going? Friday straight after school? Or Saturday afternoon?'

'Friday.'

'Is Mirry looking forward to it?' He held her hand now.

'She talks about it sometimes. She can't remember what coconut tastes like.'

They parked their car that October Friday half a mile away in a street of terraced houses where young Pakistanis stood decoratively on doorsteps, eyeing the line of limousines. From this distance they could hear the clump of the Fair, enfeebled as if bandsmen beat drums in an irregular contest of strength; as soon as the three emerged from the side road they joined other families marching downhill, all with purpose. On the boulevard, and they crossed by the metal school bridge, itself part of the adventure to the bubbling Miranda, they came across hawkers with balloons, great bunches, and now people stepped out in the heavy mud of penetrating noise. They ventured through the metal bollards, past the policeman, the St John's Ambulance tent, and into the throb of fierce enjoyment.

Every booth or ride was already lighted though it was broad day still. At this hour it was not yet crowded, but one could not comfortably stop. Above, the sky stretched brightly remote, cut by spreading vapour trails.

'What do we want?' David demanded. Miranda walked quiet now, overcome, hanging on their hands. 'A ride?' The child did not answer, eyes bright, biting her lip at a speeding rocket shrieking with metallic violence to their right. 'How about that then? Flash Star?' She shook her head, but smiled, knowing he did not mean it. 'Mexican Hat?'

They rolled 2p pieces on to easy squares and lost. Elizabeth threw a wild dart for a prize: the child chose a two-inch, ugly, hair-haloed monkey, its features gay with human imbecility. Miranda, prompted, tested the helter-skelter on her own; as she walked into the dark door she looked at them over her shoulder. They waved with a pang, but as soon as she emerged, they directed her back for a second slide. This time down she shouted with laughter.

David threw manfully at a coconut shy, hit nothing, tried again, failing.

'We shall have to buy one,' he told them. 'Shameful.'

Miranda treated herself to candyfloss, insisted that her parents taste the spun sugar. They declared delight, denied it with their faces, pleasing the child. Now David won a small ring on the rifle-range while mother and daughter rode the prancing horses, holding their twisted golden poles, as the steam organ jigged among the obliterating blare of electrical distortion. They squinted at the King of Giants, the World's Tallest Man, as he leapt, then bent to blubber lips at a small boy, who merely turned his back as if he'd noticed nothing. Still they moved uphill, where Miranda was weighed, and received a recording card with the legend on the back: 'You will marry happily but not the man of your dreams. That is the story of your life.' David tucked it into his waistcoat pocket.

'Did you marry the man of your dreams?' she asked Liz, skipping now, barely able to contain herself, straining for the next diversion.

'Of course.' The answer was lost in babel.

At the top of the hill the crowd lumped suddenly thicker, so that for a minute they could not move, but clung together, near a pile of red trestles. David could make out currents of people surging against bobbing heads, and then in no time space cleared, abounded, they could clamber down, and out, with elbow room to see the Kiss-me-quick hats, the balloons, the tawdry-topped canes. Liz shouted her hate for the pungency of hot-dog stalls; David remembered mushy peas; Miranda had had enough of her candyfloss.

Noise bothered their ears; oil burnt in the thumping diesels; shabby young men vaulted from seat to seat to compartment collecting fares, unshaven, unsmiling, sad-faced in the breath-taking racket. After a predator's wait David bundled his women into a dodgem car, and they jerked, and bumped, sparks crackling. They took a second ride, straight-faced.

David watched.

'When I was young this was the only chance most people of my sort had to drive a car.' He stood in regret. Miranda urged them towards the next excitement, thoroughly uncertain which way to drag. David accompanied her on to a dipping aeroplane that yawed and zig-zagged sickeningly. From terra firma they squinted admiringly at a madder machine that flung itself wide and screaming murderously high, blaring its crazy acceleration, shaking the squealing upright spars, the ground.

'That's not safe,' Liz said.

'I'll take your word,' he answered.

Miranda refused the Ferris wheel, rode the ghost train, to the adults a ridiculously short-lasting spin, out of the darkness in a blink, but it impressed their daughter.

'I could feel the ghost's fingers,' she said. 'Cold and wet.'

'Poor thing,' Liz said. 'Were you scared?'

'I liked it. And when that green skeleton came out, the man in front of me was kissing the girl. I thought they might have Count Dracula.'

'Drinking your blood?' asked David.

'No, yours.' She ran off for three paces, laughing.

As she walked soberly down the line of sideshows on the far side of the Fair, the sky was darkening, the garish lights flashed gaudier. David described a boxing booth, flea circuses from his youth, but now Miranda walked tiredly, refusing a toffee apple, her face peaky, pale as the fare-collectors'.

She sat in the back of the car with her mother, said she had enjoyed it, but claimed, 'it was all too much'. Would she like to go again? 'Next year,' she ventured, 'perhaps.'

When she was in bed, no dissent this night, the parents drank whisky and water, unusually.

'Did you enjoy that?' Liz asked.

'Not half bad. Did you?'

'Miranda didn't get as much out of it as I expected.'

'It's a bit overwhelming,' he said.

'She's seven. That's about the time for fairs. Then and teenage. No, she liked it, but she's half-hearted somehow; didn't you feel that?'

'No,' he said. 'I thought she was well away.'

'Perhaps it was me.'

'Are you tired, then?'

'Not really.'

He talked again about the fairs of his youth, the wakes; ragged-trousered urchins dipped and wheeled; a tanner stretched into a fortune; authorities wielding sticks retired defeated.

'What did your father say about all this?' she asked.

'He didn't know.'

'I bet he didn't.'

David looked grave at this exchange, handsome and at ease, but serious as if his present poise redeemed earlier misconduct.

'Do you ever see these schoolfriends now?'

'No. Never.'

'Not when you visited your father?'

'No. Not to the best of my recollection.'

'You don't regret that? If they were close?'

'No. Their interests and mine won't coincide, will they?'

'It's the same with your first girl-friends, is it?'

'The same.'

He was in no hurry, utterly polite, but distant so that she could not follow why he'd reminisced so long. Perhaps, no, certainly, the visit had pleased him; proud of his wife and daughter, he dredged in his memory to maintain contact with her. She looked on him with affection, told him in return that she could not remember patronizing a fair until she was grown-up.

'Did your parents not approve, then?'

'I hardly remember a fair. I suppose there must have been some somewhere, but they didn't impinge on us.'

'And a vicar's daughter had to behave?'

'That was never said once, or implied. But it's quite likely I was so conformist it didn't need saying.'

He talked again about the north, the smoke, his mother's care, demands, threats.

'She would have been pleased with you?'

'Suppose so. She would have compared me favourably with my dad.'

'Would that have been fair?'

'I've thought about that since he died. It never bothered me at the time. It seemed natural that she'd tick off Dad as well as me. I was thoroughly used to it. Jen was always delicate, needed pampering. We needed keeping up to scratch. I don't know whether she ever made head or tail of my father. He was everybody's doormat, and stubborn, his own man. Never unpleasantly. When she dusted the place, about five times daily, he just moved from chair to chair out of her way, one ahead. She wanted action and results.'

'And your father?'

'He was comfortable, with a respectable wage packet, better off than his dad. Nobody's ever satisfied. But he was near it. His engine, his allotment, his prayer meetings. And yet I don't think he was a markedly religious man. No, that's wrong. I wouldn't know. He'd been brought up to chapel, and it was enough.'

'Was he never angry?'

'Could be. Occasionally. He hated cheating. But he soon forgot. He'd a sense of his own sin rather than mine. That was typical of one kind of nonconformist. He never said this but I think he attributed Jen's death to something he'd done wrong. He wouldn't admit that; it was too barbarous. He loved his children.'

Elizabeth warmed to him, putting it down to the whisky.

12

On the Monday after the Fair Roderick Wincanton telephoned.

Elizabeth sat to her lunch of black coffee, cheese and ryvita. The new *au pair*, recently arrived from France, had the afternoon off, but would pick Miranda up from school.

'I didn't know you were staying with the Paiges. I saw Tony . . .'

'I'm ringing from the station.'

He arrived by taxi in bright sunshine, overcoat artistically open. He apologized for his intrusion, drank coffee, ate new-baked scones. His breathing was less noisy, but he looked over his shoulder, suspiciously uneasy.

'I'll be blunt with you,' he said, after twenty minutes. 'I came up on the off-chance. If you'd not been at home, I should have been driven round, walked this path, looked in your windows and sloped off. I'm superstitious.'

'Sounds intriguing,' she said. He fiddled in his trouser pockets.

'I've come to a stop,' he said, 'on both books.' She nodded. 'I wanted to see you.' She had no answer to that, but was encouraged by his healthy appearance, his firm voice, the absence of wheezing. 'I'll speak frankly. It's the only way.'

'Have another scone. You've had no lunch.'

He reached, took a mouthful, dusted his lips of flour.

'I love you,' he said. When she did not answer he continued, 'You know that?'

'No.'

'It must seem ridiculous to you. . . .' He stopped. 'I was going to say faintly ridiculous.' He grimaced, moved the bitten scone across his china plate. 'Ridiculous that someone in, well into his sixties should fall in love with a girl less than half his age. And with no encouragement on your part. What I think you won't understand is that anyone as ugly, and debilitatcd, as I am can feel as strongly as I did as a young man, more so perhaps in that there's so little possibility of physical release. But it is so. I don't know if you wish to comment.'

Taken aback she said, 'I'm flattered.'

'Desperately in love,' he smiled, tousled his hair with delicate finger, 'like a young boy. There it is. I want you to accept it as a fact. Ridiculous, as I've said. Even comical, but a fact.' Again he smiled so that fleetingly she had an idea how attractive he had been as a young man. 'I've been able to say it without histrionics. That's good. When you're here I really am on my best behaviour.' She murmured comforting noises, and looking out of her window found the leaves thick green still with the exception of one pear tree which flaunted its purplish brown. 'I can see that you're puzzled. Civilized exchanges like ours are first-rate, but . . .' He rubbed his hands now, polished off his scone, distributing crumbs.

'Tell me about your books.'

'I've started my thriller. You knew that. It went like a house on fire. Well, with my usual wet combustibles. I keep the two concurrent. Nine to twelve, serious. Two to five, entertainment, three days a week. I've never tried two pieces of fiction together, but I'm used to putting down one piece of writing and taking up another immediately. Any journalist can do it. But then the two began to interfere with each other.

149

Or that's not quite accurate. Let me put it like this.' He enjoyed himself, did not decline another scone, buttered it thickly. 'There's one matter that's occupied me, obsessed me and I used it in the thriller. What happens to the consciousness of people like me, living comfortable lives, prospering, when the Gestapo or the KGB knock you up in the middle of the night, and rush you off to the firing-squad or the labour camp. What sort of sensibility would you have left?'

'Surely, such people must suspect or fear they're proscribed?'

'Not always. There are denunciations from friends, even relatives. And confessions are made which bear no relationship to truth. Now, I had as a symbol a cat. I'm fond of cats, though I'm not allowed to keep one now. My lungs, y'know. Allergic to fur or dust, or something. The cat sits there, in the comfortable warmth of the hearthrug while the master of the house is marched off. Does it know? Presumably it sees and hears. But they're selfish creatures; that's what attracts me to them.' He drifted away from her, stared upwards, fine fingers tapping the edge of his plate.

'You mean the cat represents the rest of us?'

'If you like.' He came back. 'But it might equally be the trees growing in the garden, the clouds floating, the orchestra playing Bach on the radio. Anyhow, I used this cat in the thriller, and it made a good page or two, but then I began to think, no, I was convinced that I should have written it into the other book, in that it seemed more important than anything in that. Once I started thinking like this, I just stopped work.'

'Why didn't you cut it out of one and put it in the other?' Elizabeth had no faith in her question.

'It fitted perfectly where it was. Don't you see? The entertainment had proved itself more serious than the real book.'

'That's good, isn't it?'

'I'm afraid not. You don't see – and how could I expect you to? – how delicately balanced the distinction between success or failure is. The first often depends on the second. The second provides motive and impetus, but only if other things are right. I lost confidence. I'm mixed. I'm incapable. And so I come to see you.'

'And what will that do for you?'

'You'll be yourself, and I shall enjoy looking at you, and hearing you speak, just being yourself.'

'I can see that,' her tone chaffed, 'but when you've looked your fill, your problems haven't gone away.'

'No, but I hope I shall be confident enough to master them. All art consists in mounting obstacles, often self-imposed. After this little holiday, I'll be more energetic, available, adaptable.'

'You've been working too hard,' she said.

'Possible. I don't feel old, you know. Even when I'm ill.'

He finished his snack, and they walked together round the garden, she naming plants, he waddling in delight.

'I hadn't realized that you were such an expert.'

'My father was keen.'

'I see, I see. Do you know as I stood outside the station I had another bonus. I was unsure what to do, so before I rang, I just walked into the street. And three workmen were re-building a wall, and had a portable radio playing, a Welsh hymn, "Crug-y-Bar", or something, male voices. I listened. . . .'

'Motionless and still?'

He nodded, rapt, not listening to the quotation.

'It lifted me. My confidence stood restored. I came here, poised for the cure.'

'You'll be able to write again?'

'I shall.'

'How do you know that?' she demanded, mock-stern.

'I've composed my first two sentences. In my head.'

'One for each book?'

'No. For the proper performance.'

They walked the garden cheerfully, and now he put names, common and botanical, to the flowers. He did not drag, so that she, greatly relishing his company, invited him to stay to early dinner. He, more than delighted, sat in the kitchen as she prepared the meal, offered acceptable suggestions, washed up, made a sauce. When Miranda returned about four with the *au pair*, the cooks were laughing their heads off over their preparations. Miranda eyed them seriously.

'Did you come via the cemetery?' Elizabeth asked.

'We saw the weeping tree,' Michèle said.

Miranda was called on for explanations, so that she and Wincanton were soon engaged on competitive exaggeration, elaborating a known story. He was superlatively good, and his incidental detail, the jewelled false leg of a giant, the pond that collected angels' tears, the crook-backed white crow who nested in the weeping beech commanded Miranda's respect. She knew a master, set about making the most of him. She would suggest, in a tentative, thoughtful, dry-as-dust voice the staid beginning of a fairy tale and then sit back for his coruscations.

'Light the blue touchpaper and retire,' Liz said, in an interval.

'What are you talking about, mummy?'

'Fireworks. *Jeux d'artifice.*'

Miranda turned her back on such adult triviality, smiled at her wonder man who so brilliantly catered for the insatiate appetite. When David returned home, early this evening, he found his daughter breathless, outrun, outgunned, near to admitting delighted defeat.

'Aren't you exhausted?' Liz asked Roderick.

'Exhilarated.'

The child stayed up for early dinner, and there, at the table, behaved with composure, hardly speaking, most polite, a subdued mentor to English food for Miss Flambard. David took pride in showing off his family as they sat around polished oval mahogany, the fair, expansive Liz, the smiling, watchful *au pair*, the wide-eyed and utterly sedate daughter.

While David saw Mirry to bed, and Michèle stood in the kitchen observing the washing-up machine function perfectly, Elizabeth asked her visitor if he thought of ringing Gill.

'No. I'll take my enjoyment from your daughter.'

'Won't Gill be cross?'

'Possibly, possibly.'

'That's not good, now, is it? It wouldn't take much of an effort to lift a phone.'

'There are some things I will not do.'

'Is there trouble between you?' All innocence.

'Tony told me,' Wincanton said, subdued, not swift-tongued, 'that Gillian had made a confidante of you. If this is so, she will have given you an account of my misdemeanours, my cruelties. I in no way resent this. If it eases her mind, as it sems to, it is a small price to pay. She reports me as a bastard. I don't care.'

'Even if it's not true?'

'Since she was a girl Gillian has been nervously unbalanced. I'm not going to bore you with chapter and verse. You can either believe me or not. But that means she interpreted what happened in a thoroughly distorted way. I was not perfect, far from it, but on the other hand I was no monster. I have heard from people in whom she has confided how I beat her mother, deserted them, left them poverty-stricken.'

'You didn't beat your wife?'

'I did not say that. Two or three times, at most, I became so exasperated that I resorted to a blow. Not nearly so often as she attempted violence against me. I see I've shocked you.'

'Yes.'

'It was rare, almost non-existent. Gillian saw me strike Ruth once, on one occasion only. The provocation was great.

I don't recall the incident with any sort of pride; in fact I'm bitterly sorry, but . . . That's it. But. It did her harm, perhaps, but the harm was already there.' He smiled, pensively. 'You don't know whether to believe me, do you?'

'It seems awful, anyway.' Liz could not understand how so suddenly she felt physically ill. Could keel over, heave.

'If I need to apologize,' Wincanton maintained urbanity, 'and I suppose I need, then I make my offering to you. The wound in Gillian's consciousness was not so precious – no, what am I saying? – not so conspicuous as now. I did not realize how serious her case was.'

'Why not?'

'You're suggesting I ought to have known? Perhaps so. I am selfish, and had my way to make. Not so selfish as Gillian, with whom it was almost pathological. It's difficult. Teenage daughters disappear behind bedroom doors or sulks. There are unreported conversations with mothers. As long as father provides pecuniary support. . . .'

'You did that?' Elizabeth intervened over quickly.

'Did what?'

'Act generously towards her?'

Wincanton narrowed his eyes.

'She claims otherwise, does she?' he said.

'No. She does not.' Elizabeth lied vehemently, brusque.

'I thought I did. Again I may be wrong. I may have misjudged her expectations.'

'Come now.' Her waggish finger warned. 'You'd know that.'

'She had a dress allowance. I can't remember what it was. They left me out of these affairs.'

'And you resented it?'

'I was glad.'

David appeared expansively to invite them both upstairs, especially 'Mr Man', for a final session with Miranda.

The child sat upright, in dressing-gown, an adult book

open on her coverlet.

'What's that, then?' Wincanton asked mock-seriously.

'Guess.' Miranda already laughed.

'*Pride and Prejudice.*'

'*Stories of Robin Hood, the Bowman*, by H. Arnot Widdowes.'

' 'Ow 'arrowing,' he said.

'Sometimes I think you're mad.' The child delivered judgement in a matter-of-fact tone.

'Or sad, or bad, or just like dad,

'Or fed or dead, or down in bed,' he intoned.

'Say me a poem,' she commanded.

> ' "If a man who turnips cries
>   Cry not when his father dies
>   This is proof that he had rather
>   Have a turnip than his father." '

'That's silly. I want you to say a proper grown-up poem.' Elizabeth warned her not to be rude, overexcited. 'Say me a real poem. Please. Even if I can't understand. Do you know one?'

'I do.'

'Say it for me, please.'

Wincanton looked round the bedroom without haste for the correct spot. Once he'd chosen, he stepped across and stood there, ten feet from the child, with his back to the tall doll's house, his right hand in his trouser pocket, his right foot, pointing down, over the left. Liz turned; with amusement she noted her husband had positioned himself by Mirry's pillow. No one spoke. Wincanton removed the right foot, and planted it squarely eighteen inches from the other, clasped his hands together. He kept them waiting, and yet his breathing was inaudible; he smiled without patronizing, teaching them the worth of his performance before he began it. He announced no title. The author went unnamed. He

dipped his head, and the easy, resonant voice commanded:
'Behold her single in the field.' He completed the recitation
slowly, as if he were himself improvising, or remembering the
incident in words that dropped naturally into verse. The
grown-ups waited for the child to pronounce, but she seemed
bemused, pulling but not moving her duvet.

'Did that do?' Wincanton said, striding across.

'Thank you.' Miranda appeared to have given up the world,
to be staring far off. The three watched. ' "Breaking the
silence of the seas," ' she said.

' "Among the farthest Hebrides," ' he finished it for her,
without condescension.

'Yes.' Mirry smiled. 'Thank you.'

'Are you going to cuddle down?' Liz asked.

'Not yet?' A pert eye strengthened the question. 'I'll read.
Kisses, then.' David bent first, then the mother.

'Am I included?' Wincanton was accepted with a nod. He
had trouble with his bending, but their lips touched.

'Thank you,' he said.

'Not too long now.' Liz, last through the door. Downstairs
Wincanton refused a drink, demanded a taxi, was driven to
the station by David. Miranda, asleep in no time, with the
light still on, lay neatly happy, legs bent, hair spread in fair
fuzz. Her expression was open, free but thoughtful.

David returned sooner than his wife expected.

'Did you see him on the train?'

'No. He wouldn't have me wait.' David looked into his
briefcase. 'He went down a bomb with missy, there.'

'What an expression.'

'Don't you approve? Of him, not my phraseology. He said
that poem in a remarkable way. Who wrote it?' She told him.
'Have we got a copy? Do you know, Liz, it was well, superior.
As if you'd invited Yehudi Menhuin to practise in your par-
lour. I think Mirry knew that. It silenced her. She'd been
laughing and jumping and wrestling with me.'

'You'd tired her out.'

'He knew exactly what to do. That doesn't often happen.' He rubbed his face, boardroom serious. 'He didn't put it on at all. It was there, and yet it was remarkable. As if he were more than the sum of the parts, if you understand me.'

'He's a very experienced lecturer.'

'He seemed, this is what I'm saying, a quite different person from the man I took down to the station. That's not exaggeration, is it? I seem to remember Gill telling me he won the DSO. Is that right?'

'Look him up in *Who's Who*.'

'I will tomorrow. I thanked him for the poem, and he said, "I stagger from one hypocrisy to another." '

'And what do you think that meant?'

'That this was only a performance, that he didn't feel it deeply, that he regretted fooling us into believing he did, and that his whole life was a series of such deceptions.'

'Maybe.' Liz was impressed with the explanation. 'Did he mention Gillian?'

'Not a word.'

'He wouldn't ring her up. Did she ever tell you he was the cause of her troubles?'

'Not that I recall. She played that down, rather.' He looked up to fathom the effect of his quizzical sentence, adverb, on her. When she made no reply other than opening her book again, he said, 'Mirry was impressed, hypocrite or not.'

'He seems to know his way round. She was fond of your father.'

'He was a relative.'

'Oh, don't be stupid. Sorry. I mean, that wouldn't affect her, would it?'

'I think so.' The northern voice held its rebuke. 'If only because she knew what we expected of her. I would never have thought of a poem.'

'She asked for it.'

'Out of the blue, and he was ready. Not half-prepared. He silenced us.'

'Wordsworth did.'

'As you will. He knew, then, what Wordsworth would do.'

Her husband said no more, but sat preoccupied, unable to give himself a satisfactory explanation, lifting his papers from the table, returning them, flattening them with a wide spread of hand. Within ten minutes he had recovered, concentrated on his reports or whatever. But he worked down here, in company, and it pleased her, unreasonably.

13

Miranda went down with influenza just before the half-term holiday, scotching a seaside holiday in Devon. The child tossed in high fever, pink-faced and sweaty, fretful, unable to settle comfortably.

'Her temperature will be down tomorrow, don't you worry,' the doctor promised.

On that first evening Elizabeth had talked to her husband, an ear cocked for the child above. It seemed that while both listened for a sniffle or cry from the bedroom, they could question each other, because their main attention was elsewhere. Recalling the exchanges, Liz barely believed David had been so free with information.

He did not talk, regularly or often, at length about his work, because it was, unless one was deeply involved, he claimed, and one had mastered swathes of detail, pointlessly boring. Tonight he explained how they had decided to make a small, complicated component for an aircraft engine manufacturer.

'Why didn't they make their own?'

'Not worth it. It needed an outlay of too much capital. They weren't prepared.' The explanation was punctuated by pauses for listening. 'They'd something nearly as good, but they argued if we could come up with the component it would be used in a further two or three developments, and could have what their man called a hundred and one spin-offs. That's true enough in this line. So we put our experts on to it, with their man; we had him over and they set about him; he was really bright, and then we knocked this bit out inside a few months. Then came the testing. That was successful, more so than expected, and so it comes before the financial boys.'

'Is that you?'

'Not really. Perhaps so. I still think of myself as an engineer. We ask them how many they'll want this year, and next, and next. And then we cost the setting up of the plant, and the wages.'

'That will give you the price?' she asked.

'In the normal way. Not this time. We should lose money for at least three years, even at a price we could hope to get. But our metallurgists and designers were keen this round, one because they'd got an interesting bit of metal, and two they had the chance to set up a completely mechanized assembly line, very small, of course, but run by cassettes, not human brains. They love that, and don't often get the chance to do it properly. We have to make use of the machines we've got, and then the unions have to be informed. Properly too. I'm not blaming them. It's their job to look after their members. But our boys said they could solve every foreseeable problem in robot processes on this bit of hanky-panky set up down twenty-odd yards of factory.'

'So you decided?'

'We have a meeting. We decide what we shall lose, as lose we shall. Then the experts argue their case against questions, especially accountants' questions. They'd already submitted written briefs.'

'How long does this take?'

'A morning. No more. Though it's new we've seen equivalent problems. We tell the unions what we're up to, what we want.'

'Are they awkward?'

'No. Why should they be?'

'It might put all their members out of work when you've decided in two or three years to replace the whole of one of your factories with machine-operated machines.'

'They'd argue the case, then. They're pragmatic. Like the management. We all look ahead, but we don't know when and how the impetus will come to set us on something really radical. We try bits and bobs, like this. That's all an efficient firm like ours can do. It's more like the old bike shop round the corner than you'd think.'

'No wonder we're stagnating.'

'We aren't. By no means. You'd be surprised how much money we're piling up from the good old traditional lines.'

'Profitably?'

'Yes. We're still making profit. Not as much as we'd like, but not nothing. And this little experiment, and one or two more like it, might be the next big money-spinners. We're old-style traders, hobbled by the strong pound or some foreign competition, but we've sharp operators, and we're big enough to have our hooks out in new streams. Not a bad life. We could be caught out, like the Swiss watchmakers, by some development, but I can't guess what it is likely to be.'

'And you're a sharp operator?'

'Yes. That's it. If I can't guess, nobody else can.'

'Boast, boast.'

A whimper from upstairs had both quiet, and, repeated, on their feet.

'My turn,' he said.

'No. I'll go. I'd rather.'

'I'll warm the coffee.'

The exchange had pleased and when next day she sat at the bedside of the livelier Miranda, she felt she'd learned from her husband. Every two or three months he'd go out of his way to say something about the firm; it was sometimes quite explicit, a detailed description of a process or product, more often as last night a comment on how they thought, but all a warming expression of confidence in her, her ability to understand, her right to be told. As she listened, at dinner parties, to other directors, to guests, they lacked David's purpose, in that they talked to convince themselves or dazzle her. He won her attention, earned it, without pyrotechnics. His colleagues wanted, badly wanted, her admiration; he shared himself with her.

'Where's Daddy today?'

'Flying to Scotland.'

'He came in to see me. I was just lying there.'

'What did he say?'

'He asked me if I was better. And he gave me a drink.'

'That was good.'

'Lemonade with three ice cubes in it.'

'Three?'

'Yes. And I said, "Is it better than they'll give you on the aeroplane?"'

'What did he say, darling?'

' "Not so strong."'

Though the child looked peaky and did not ask about coming downstairs she made excitement out of the small early exchange with her father.

David did not return until the next day, sat upstairs for an hour with his daughter, but appeared lethargic and preoccupied over the dinner table. After the *au pair* went out to her class, Elizabeth parked him in front of the television with a glass of whisky. Inside ten minutes he was asleep, quite still, with nothing restive about him, chin down, fast away but soundlessly, without snuffle or snore. His hair stood in spikes at his crown, lending a boyish air; she could well imagine his going up thus for an attendance prize at Sunday school. He woke swiftly forty minutes later, sat straight, eyed her brightly as she read a novel; the television dazzled its colours silently behind her.

'I'm never here when I'm wanted,' he said.

'Go on.'

'When Mirry was really ill. She frightened me Monday night, when she was so feverish. I felt helpless. You looked pretty,' he screwed a frown, 'composed.' She didn't answer. He scratched his right temple then smoothed his jets of hair with the flat of a hand. 'I'll tell you something,' he said.

She waited.

'I did something I hadn't done for a long time. I prayed for her.'

'What did you say?' Contained surprise.

' "Please God look after Miranda." '

'No more?'

'No.' He seemed glad it was out, perhaps about it.

'And that's unusual for you, I take it?'

'Yes.' Lips thin, he looked at the barely touched whisky.

' "I pray, for fashion's word is out,

And prayer comes round again",' she quoted.

'Who said that?'

'Yeats. Did it do any good, do you think?'

'Impossible to decide, isn't it? But it established the right balance, between God and me. Look at it like this: if God exists, that's about all I'm entitled to ask Him.'

'Why? The more Mirry wanted from you, the better pleased you'd be.'

'Pride. My pride. If I were God, I wouldn't mind that much. It's reasonable.'

She laughed, in joy, but shakily.

'And when you'd done it . . . ?'

'I said it again.'

'In case He didn't hear, or didn't recognize you?'

'To convince myself I'd said it.' He rubbed his hands. 'Though that is what I wanted to do, I had to convince myself I'd done it. It's complicated, isn't it?'

They took another drink together, and said no more.

Gillian Paige arrived two days later with the news that her father had finished his thriller, had promised, had insisted on giving her a look at the typescript, had found his work good.

'Last time I saw him he was stuck,' Liz said.

'That's why I'm to tell you. You made him write, he says. Not that he's ever short of words. He wanted to visit you. Period. Now he's over the moon.'

'You weren't angry that he didn't call in on you?'

'No. Typical. Selfish as hell. Not that I want to see him. But Joel Compton, his agent, says this will make a packet.'

'Is that likely?'

'Shouldn't be surprised,' Gill said. 'He's talented. Twisted, and clever. Twisted because clever, perhaps. But he insisted I came over. You're responsible, blah-blah.'

'Aren't you excited for him?'

'In moderation.'

'Do you remember saying that he always wrote about his own hang-ups, but in a disguised way? Will this be the same?'

'Did I? Maybe.'

Gillian looked out towards the garden where afternoon died in a silvery light, the pale moon outlandish among triangular scones of cloud. Clearly her interest had disappeared.

'What about his other book? The serious one?'

'What other book? He's always writing something. I don't keep up with him.'

'Why did he promise you a typescript?' Liz demanded.

'Search me. He's cracked. He wouldn't want to impress me,

that I will say. I just don't know; I just don't care. Perhaps he thought I'd lend it to you.' Gillian spoke with a childish emphasis, as if she could kick furniture or wiggle rude fingers at her nose-end. She left soon after, refusing all hospitality, ashamed of her visit, testy with herself, but uncertain.

Sir Roderick himself telephoned to ask if he could dedicate the book to her, and at that she was much taken, almost believing his flatteries. Their twenty-minutes conversation left her singing round the house. When half an hour later Anthony Paige rang asking for a short interview, she spoke so cheerfully that she felt she'd overdone it, spoilt her image with him.

Paige appeared after lunch; she reported her conversation with Wincanton.

'You've had about enough of our family, then.' He spoke through closed lips, humming, the smile at his eyes mere fine wrinkles. 'Still, I'm here. I don't know why I've come. Did you find Gill more settled when she came in the other day?'

Liz assented. 'She complains, of course. Nothing will ever be perfect for her. But Roddy had been on to her about his book, and the pair of 'em seem to be making it up between them. She runs him down, but she seemed pleased, with him at least. And this is part of an all-round improvement. Usually, if she praises somebody, it's at the expense of someone else. She's been talking to me. Nothing much, about shopping or Christmas or my mother's cats, but just like everybody else, or what I imagine everybody else is like. Until this morning.'

He refused a drink, but stood up, took a step or two, laying the flat of his fingers on a sideboard, lifting them to touch a cascade of small ivy leaves, then to pluck at the cloth of his elbow with a conjuror's regularity so that she expected him to end with a fool's gold handful of small change. Wanly smiling he sat down. She waited, wishing they had glasses or china to occupy themselves with.

'She gave me an account of a dream over breakfast. You perhaps remember that one of the Sundays ran a photo feature on that religious sect that murdered visiting American VIPs and then wiped itself out. South America. Guyana. Some mad black parson left a tape recorder playing. And then there were photographs. Horrible, really, but they might have been on the beach or the parks on bank holiday, people in coloured shorts, lying there, taking a nap, arms round the children.'

'I saw it.'

'She poked round with it for days. Wish I'd seen the damn thing first, but I can't go censoring every bit of newsprint that comes into the house.' He bit his knuckle hard, at length. 'She made a remark or two, at the time, that was all. I kept my eyes and ears open, but it passed. I was pleased. If she could put up with that, she'd stand anything. Then, this morning; well. She dreamed she took part in some such mass suicide. Her family, and yours, were in it, she thought. A dozen or so people. And some children. But she wasn't sure. Your Miranda is the only child in the family, and she couldn't swear she was there. She thought she was. She said she concentrated entirely on herself, what she felt.'

'I see.' Paige seemed to expect an interruption. 'Where did this take place?'

'That's odd. In a primary school yard, in Highgate, where she went first, at five. She hadn't thought about the place for years. It was a bright day with blue sky. Like Guyana. And there were no spectators, nobody looking on.'

'Was I there?'

'She thinks so, though she's not certain. She doesn't know if I was there. But they were walking about a bit, or we were, and then all lay down on the tarmac or whatever.'

'Why were we . . .?'

'She didn't say. It seemed right, sensible enough, even if frightening. There seemed a good enough reason, somewhere. You know how it is in dreams. You'd think that was the most important matter, but it wasn't. It was accepted. Down they got in the school yard, in the sunshine, to die.'

'Were there no speeches?'

'One. Your husband stood there while the rest were lying down, and told them the effect of the poison. She can't remember what the poison was, nor its effect, except that it wasn't violent. There were no convulsions. That had shocked her about this American affair, the parents holding on to, holding down the children who were writhing. But here there were no spasms, David said, one just passed off. It frightened her, because she felt there would be chest pains, but he wasn't arguing with anyone, merely informing them, in a dry-as-dust way, with that voice of his when he's making something clear.'

'Did they take the poison?'

'No. She woke up, very confused, she said, but determined to hang onto her dream. She usually forgets, but she made herself go over this one, remember the details.'

'And David was the leader?'

'Not really. Or only in so far as he knew about the science. There was no attempt, she said, to argue or coerce them, us into agreement. That seems to have been decided before the dream began. When they were walking about in the school-yard she was sure they had made their minds up.'

'Was she frightened?'

'Terrified. It seemed an awful thing. She was afraid, too, of possible pain, but the fact that there seemed no reason for the action, nor that they were doing it publicly so that anyone walking past in the street could have looked over the wall or railings and seen what they were up to.'

'Nobody did?'

'It seems not. Another thing was that the ground didn't seem uncomfortable. Have you ever tried lying flat on hard ground? It fairly bangs your head even when you're lying still. But they lay there, and your husband, standing, explained to the one or two near him, no raising of voice, what the poison would do to them.'

'It upset her.'

'She said she was afraid. In a silent, paralysed way, both in the dream and afterwards, but she was determined to hang on to the details.'

'Why was that?'

'I honestly don't know, but she's no fool, and in some ways she's obstinate. She'd decided it was important, and was determined not to let go.'

'But there are gaps? She's vague, you say, about who was there, and why they'd made the pact, and what the poison was.'

'Isn't this always the case with dreams? And besides,' Tony opened his eyes slowly wide, 'she was concentrated entirely on herself. That's what she said. And it's exactly what she's like in real life.'

They sat looking away from each other.

'I'm going to have a cup of coffee,' Liz said, finally, barely coughing up words out of her chest. 'Will you?' He nodded, eyes wet, as if he'd altogether abandoned his voice. Elizabeth, glad to be alone in the kitchen, dawdled with kettle, water, tray, cups, beans, grinder. When she returned, in not much over five minutes, he seemed not to have moved so that for a minute she played with the frozen fantasy that he had poisoned himself, as he sat, that his recital had been a prelude to this uncomfortable, up-sitting death.

He congratulated her on the coffee, back to smart nor-mality, but was soon apologizing for bothering her.

'You see, I don't understand it. It frightened her, and that's why she wanted to remember it, but it doesn't explain any-thing, does it now? I can't help wondering if it's not the prelude to something?'

'Such as?'

'Suicide.' He seemed to come out with that.

'Has she tried before?'

'Not sure.' He sounded shifty. 'Not sure really. I know that sounds crazy, but it's about how it is.' He thinned his lips, prepared to add nothing. 'It's not a question of breaking confidence.' He concentrated on his cup.

They talked about Roderick Wincanton's new book, and there he confessed that he'd no idea of the subject matter.

'She clams up on me. It's as if she's guarding his secrets from me. I don't want to know, if she doesn't want to let on. But I make conversation, because it keeps her off her hook. But they phone each other pretty well every day, and she's written letters.'

'Is it good?'

'It's never happened before. You can't tell. We've had so many ups and downs recently that I began to wonder what it means if she exchanges more than a word with the milkman.'

'That must be awful.'

'Not pleasant, no.' He smiled, impudently, for him. 'But not boring. Are you going away? Just now? Or at Christmas? You'll come up and see us, won't you?'

'We greatly enjoyed our visit.'

'You'll come?'

'Yes, but we need to give David plenty of notice.'

'He drives himself, that man. My parents are always talking about you. I think they'd like to invite you, but daren't.' He smiled broadly. 'They admire you both. My father's on about you at every verse end.'

'He knows a good thing when he sees it,' she said. He'd said much the same of his wife.

'That's how he'd praise himself.'

Tony thanked her again when he left, saying that she probably didn't realize what a relief it gave him to 'say his piece'. 'Your husband there, just flatly outlining the ins and outs of the poison worried me, I can tell you.'

'Gill forgot it.'

'She didn't forget that it wouldn't hurt, nor the way he delivered his information, nor who it was who spoke.' The cold seriousness of his voice alarmed her, before the tone changed, brightened. 'Thanks for everything.'

Elizabeth watched him cross the garden, noticing that though he never glanced back, he carefully closed and fastened the white gates. His hair blew in the sunshine.

14

Gillian Paige and Elizabeth Watson met several times by appointment in the next few weeks. Gill made the first moves, exerted herself to be pleasant, spoke about her father's success or her own Christmas preparations with moderate but sincere pleasure; her husband too was not excluded from the distribution of praise. Now Gill, though she dressed strikingly as ever, in bright red silks, black, once a wide-brimmed hat like a predatory bird perching, made no feverish claims for her information with 'It's odd' or 'The most curious thing I ever saw'; she now had sentences which held inherent interest.

On a silvery morning in November – it had rained heavily in the night and even now smudges of grey-black cloud hurried off – as the two women walked round the Paiges' garden, Gill stopped, her gloved hand tracing the rounded top of a leafless dwarf lilac, and said, 'I should like to see the east coast. I've never been. Will you go with me?'

'For how long?'

'A day. It takes only a bit over two hours.'

It seemed a foolish idea at this time of the year, but so easily arranged that Elizabeth, consulting her diary and demanding a delayed decision, agreed to go. They travelled the flat way, via Boston, and admired the great church-tower of St Botolph's.

'Not what I'd call a "Stump",' Elizabeth demurred. 'I wish I had my camera.'

'Rod says one should never take a camera in a new place. It makes you idle. You won't look properly, think it's done for you.'

'What does he do, then?'

'Takes notes. Stands there scribbling in a big desk diary. And adds to that when he's back in his hotel.'

'He's a worker?'

'Nobody said otherwise. He used his eastern notebooks again in this new novel. Said they were priceless. I guess he's got photographs as well.'

'What's it about?'

'The book. Drug smuggling and spying. That's very complicated. And there are antiques in it.' They stood on a bridge, on a grey Lincolnshire morning, and traffic swished, braked, clanked behind them. 'It's about friendship and betraying one's country. But there are all sorts of good things in it. There's a trip up-river to somewhere near the Burma–Assam border that's marvellous. You're there. I didn't want him to stop describing. The agent, James Scholar, was being chased, and that was exciting enough, but nothing like the mud, or the fierce waters, the climbs, the jungle growth. He made a new world. It's just me, perhaps. Other people will like the chases and fights and blood and sex, but I really admired the leaves and bamboos and bushes.'

'And is his hero interesting?'

'He's got this funny name. Scholar.'

'As if he's learning?' Liz asked.

'Yes. He was brought up in China. He's a missionary's son. But he's no sexual morals. Only his friendship. For an official. They were in the army together. And he's a double agent, the official, out of conviction. Has that spoilt it for you?'

'Not at all.'

'And Scholar's got a Chinese son, or a son by a Chinese woman. And he's in it. He hates his father. And he's got no country, doesn't speak English properly, or not at all – I forget. But there are some marvellous things. You tell me, Liz,' now the eyes stared, 'why Rod is better at mud than morals. Or why I think so.'

'I'd have to read it first.'

The tension on Gill's face eased, and they made their way back to the car, arm in arm, and out to the flat roads, the ditches, the dull Rembrandt houses, the enormous sky. Gillian laughed a good deal, talking about her father's book, and especially an incident in Hong Kong that was both hilarious and frightening, when Scholar was tailed for the wrong reasons.

'It really was clever, because though it frightens, and seems ridiculous at the same time, all the clues are there so that you can deduce what's happening. Not that anybody will.'

'Do you know what I think?' Liz asked, unhurriedly driving. 'You greatly admire your father, for all you say.'

'I don't deny it. Specially now he's going to make some money.'

'Do you remember telling me that he wrote about his hangups?'

'Did I?'

'Has he done so here?'

'Let's see now.' Gillian wriggled, but within limits. Elizabeth had insisted that she fasten her seat belt. 'That would be about right.'

'Go on, then. Explain.'

'Well, he's devious. He can't do anything straight. If you sent him to the nearest shop to buy a pint of milk, he'd have some excuse for going to two different places to get halves. So this sort of story suits. And then it's out East. He's never come to terms with that.'

171

'The war, do you mean?'

'And after.'

'But he won the DSO.'

'Did he tell you?' Gill asked, affronted.

'No, he did not. David told me, I think. He'd looked him up.'

'Careful, careful David. He needs a book to tell him. But Roddy's main trouble is duty, especially to people. Especially to us, his family. That's what cuts into him. And he's divided. Patriotism and friendship. He dumps one, keeps one. But he hates both, because they make demands a selfish man like him can't answer. That's why it's so good. When you know what to do, and can't manage it, then you're well set up for a book, because you'll feel all the pulls and drawbacks.'

'You need talent.'

'He's got that. And practice. He's done his duty by the written word. But it's the ferocity of his moral conflicts . . .'

'You'll be telling me next that only the wicked can write novels.'

'We're all wicked. We all do wrong. And a novelist just uses his imagination to magnify, to exaggerate. Nobody's without a sense of falling short.'

'You're a proper puritan,' Liz said.

'Any daughter of Rod's would have a sense of sin.'

'Would she be against it, though?'

'Sometimes,' Gill spoke slowly, but pleasantly as the flat dull land scudded insipidly by, 'I think you've had life too easy. I don't know, mind you. Your parents are both dead, aren't they? I don't know. Perhaps I shouldn't have said that. I always put my foot in it.'

'Don't apologize. That spoils it.' Silly generosity.

'How was it, well, what did you think when David was going to leave you?'

Liz braked fast, as a cat, belly low, crossed the road from a cottage to opposite tumbledown huts. Gill swore at the jolt, shrieking. The driver, in control, it seemed, licked her lips, and easily resumed her former pose and pace. 'Stupid creature,' she said. 'There can't be more than half-a-dozen cars a day at this time of year, and it has to choose that minute to go on its walk-about.'

'Some people are born unlucky,' Gillian.

'Are you one of them?'

'Not of necessity. No. Not altogether.'

It silenced them, so that the humming of tyres on the roads proved conversation enough, until they reached the coast. Liz felt the incident in shoulders, arms, belly, thighs, as mild scars, warnings, portents of ill luck, and these occupied her. When they had parked the car, they strolled a hundred yards along the deserted promenade, stopping frequently to rest their hands on the low wall and then stare out across the sea, which flopped sluggishly, grey-grey green under a sky stretched in unbroken dullness.

'Is it worth coming?' Liz asked her companion.

'Oh, yes. The sea air. Just to breathe.'

'No ships.'

'No people.'

'Only us.'

'Connoisseurs.' The waves slapped, small and reluctant; the visitors could not decide whether the tide came in or went out; it seemed as uncertain itself. The women made their way to a pub, drank bitter-lemon, ate rough-hewn sandwiches, warmed their hands on coffee cups. They hardly spoke but the landlord switched on the lights over their table; the two or three drinkers at the far side of the room talked in whispers, backs hunched, apparently afraid to touch their glasses. Elizabeth roused herself and the two went out again, and set off northwards along the front.

'It's not too cold,' she encouraged.

They passed the lines of beach huts which stood uncouth in the grey light, the bright stripes, the yellows and crimsons, the white darkened, pitted, stained, Mon Abri, Us Two, Sun Trap, The Bower, Doss House, Mabel's, North Sea View, High Living, Hyde Park Corner, Sea Side, The Last Post, Solitude, Shangri-la. The two enjoyed the sound of their heels on the concrete, were lifted in an exhilaration as the sand-coloured, small waves receded. Marine clichés were exchanged; gulls swooped and called creakily. Gillian in the middle of some *sotto voce* fluency about the infinite variation of light on water stopped suddenly and placed her fingers in the crook of Elizabeth's arm. Liz stopped, looking out seawards, saw nothing of note, returned her attention to Gillian who had parted her lips in a breathless fervour, eyes delighted under the black energetic plume of her hair.

'Well?'

'You never answered my question.' Gill's expression, of expectation, ardour even, did not change.

'Sorry. I wasn't listening. I was elsewhere.'

'I don't mean just now.'

Elizabeth turned back to the sea, puzzled.

'In the car,' Gill said. 'Just before the cat. I asked you what you thought when David left you.'

The woman, elegantly made up, striking, even beautiful, with her hand out still touching her companion's arm, was mad. The ardent face spelt lunacy.

'You don't mind my asking, do you?' She laid her head to one side like a child.

Elizabeth decided to answer, ran over words. The two set off *en route*.

'It wasn't so much a case of thinking,' she said. 'I was pretty incapable of that. It was feeling, nothing outside pain.'

'I'm often like that.'

'I felt badly injured, so that whatever I did hurt me. To decide what we needed for lunch, to make up my mind to do housework. I took Miranda to the Castle Museum and I was like a walking corpse except for violent suffering.'

'Was it physical?'

'To some extent. But it impregnated my brain. That sounds silly.'

'I understand all right. Did the child notice?'

'I don't think so. Why should she? She's full of her own concerns, and, anyway she expects me to be quiet. But I was in such a mess I don't know whether I'd have noticed what she saw or didn't.'

'You don't mind telling me this?' Gillian asked.

'I hate it.'

'Because I was the cause?'

'Because I was so badly hit. I want to be less vulnerable, to be my own woman, not dependent on any man. Or woman. But it was like being in some extreme of weather, in the Arctic, where everything you do and think is modified, and regulated, and determined by the cold. I want to be temperate, not numbed or stabbed silly by what I can't control.'

They were still walking smartly in step, and the sharp movements made these statements, accurate or not, easier to enunciate.

'I'm often like that,' Gillian, breathlessly, as if she found the pace too hectic, 'but the really frightening thing is that it's about nothing, or next to nothing. You had a real reason. Your husband was deserting you and his daughter. You'd have to change your way of life, and that would create anxiety with anybody. But because somebody slights me, or I drop something, and I'm tense before my period, I go mad. Just as you describe it. In extremities. Pained. Agonized. Inside and out.'

The voice gathered strength, hectored, with breath enough now.

'I thought you were a lot better?'

'I am. I've been really steady for weeks. But how long will it last?'

They stopped, as if in collusion, to watch the buff-grey tide creep and slop round a wooden breakwater yards out, beyond unbright streaks of runnels, flat polished dullness of pools, left stranded by the idle sea.

' "The moving waters in their priestlike task

Of pure ablution round earth's human shores",' Liz quoted. It seemed utterly inappropriate once she'd mouthed it.

'That's good. Who wrote it?'

'Keats.'

'Say it again.' She did, and they watched the low, spittle-foam-edged sea. 'It sounds marvellous. Does it make sense, though? Human shores? Doesn't it wash . . .?' She flipped her hand to her side, abstracted. Liz attempted no exegesis.

'Forward, madam. Another few yards, then about turn. We've homes to go to, haven't we?'

'Some of us.' Gillian seemed momentarily colourless, barely existent.

Their cheeks glowed when they sat in the car ready for the return journey.

'I don't think this is a place I'd retire to,' Liz said, fastening her seat belt.

'You'll end up in the Seychelles.'

'I shan't, you know.'

Gillian thought her father would have liked to live abroad, but hadn't done quite well enough; the new book might change things. 'You can't guess with him.'

'Does this new book surprise you?'

'Not at all. Now he's written it, it's just what I'd expect. I didn't see that at the time, I admit. If you'd asked me before he'd written this, I'd have described the wrong sort of book, but now, this is exactly him.'

'It's exotic?'

'Yes. And violent. And unpleasant. He'd enjoy bloody

murders. There's a horribly detailed picture of a man who committed suicide by holding a handgrenade to his chest. Turns you over.'

'That's typical?'

'I think so. He must have killed people in the war.' The flat roads sang past in the darkening afternoon; the car moved comfortably fast.

'You don't know that for certain?' Liz hinted.

'No, I don't. That's one thing I've never dared to ask him. I used to want to when I was twelve or thirteen, younger, perhaps. I never could.'

'Would he have been angry?'

'You could never tell. One day he'd pull my leg about a thing, or tell the truth, and another he'd have blazed into a temper and taken it out of me for a week. What you'd call incalculable, our friend. Volatile.' Gillian laughed and made much of an examination of her fingernails. 'It's odd to me that there must be hundreds of old men like Rod walking the streets who've killed other humans, shot them, or dropped bombs on them, and yet they plod about puffing and blowing, or laying the law down or preaching and voting Conservative. They never say anything about it.'

'They consider they did their duty.'

'You think they did right?'

'I wasn't born. They'd think so.'

'Do you?'

'Since you press me. Yes. That was a just war.'

Gillian laughed again, and occupied herself winding the window up and down.

'They've experience that no young man has had.'

'Or will have, we hope,' Liz interrupted.

'Except for these terrorist bombers and murderers.' The window, addressed all this while, was now adjusted. 'They get over it. Rod has. Don't you think? They forget. They become ordinary. Perhaps all murderers would, given time.'

'Something in that. But these were socially approved killings. They won medals.'

'You're a remarkable woman, aren't you?'

'Thanks. In what way?'

'Difficult to put a finger on it. You're extraordinary when you're being very ordinary. Something like that. If I don't understand it, you don't. You're beautiful. That's at the bottom of it. I'm embarrassing you. Will you stop when we get to this wood?'

Liz, caught out, asked her companion to repeat the instruction. She drew up off the road at the side of the copse which stretched not more than forty by a hundred yards.

'Come on out,' Gill called. 'This is a call of Nature with a capital, not nature. Lock the car.'

'Throw away the key?'

Gill gaped startled at that, but pushed ahead.

'This is private,' she said. 'I wonder why it's left. Is it a windbreak, do you think? Is it any use or just a bit of atavism?' The sky had begun to darken between the boles and the ragged brambles and the saplings were rusty, haphazard, but almost cheerfully, leapings and twistings of life, leafless, but denying the wintry light, the dryness of the stems.

'Leaf mould,' Liz said, kicking into the turf. 'Your father could describe this.'

' "For in that sleep of death what dreams may come." ' Gill intoned, the thespian.

'*Hamlet*.'

'Did it for "A" level.'

'Why do you quote it?' Liz asked, thinking of Tony's recital.

'I get horrible dreams. Nightmares. I wake up screaming.'

'About what?'

'Death. Chases. Falling. Suffocating.'

'Are your father and Tony in them?'

'Sometimes.'

'Is David?'

Gillian did not answer immediately, trudged on until she reached the hedge bounding the wood where she turned left.

'No,' she said. 'Why do you ask that?' Not stopping.

'He was involved with you.'

'Involved. Involved.' Gill tramped. 'He was. And you know what I feel like. I'm glad you do. You described it properly. Not like doctors. They have no idea, though they must have listened to thousands trying to communicate it, to tell them. It angers me. But you know.' She delivered this ahead of her, but the stillness of the wood allowed each word perfection of clarity; the coldness of the air steamed in the breath, and Liz stumbling behind shivered her fear, perhaps as in a dream of following a talking scarecrow. 'You can be my friend.' Her pace increased; twigs cracked underfoot. Liz pressed to keep up for it seemed important. 'You help me. You do, don't you?' They followed a gap, came out by the car. 'Let's walk round again.'

'Why?' Liz asked.

'It does good.' Two cars flashed by on the road. 'I have to make things. Not things. Landmarks. To stand out. To pass my time. To remember myself by. I dragged you out to the sea, didn't I?' Liz thought the gloved hands would rise, grab her by the collar, and haul her again. 'You came out of kindness, or fun, or curiosity. I came to save myself.'

'By walking round this copse?'

'Why not?' Gill smiled. 'I don't have to commit murder to remember the day. I shan't forget. You think this is extreme behaviour. You know how I feel, because your husband walked out, and smashed your life. And this is how I fight my feeling, by doing something, looking for something, searching in a bit of a wood in the Lincolnshire wolds.'

'What will you find?'

'I don't know. What word would you use?'

Eliot's line presented itself in Elizabeth's head, but she

kept her mouth clamped shut. 'Distraction distracting from distraction.' Gill's chin was pressed into the fur of her short coat, but askew, cricking her neck.

'I tell you what,' Liz spoke flatly, 'you talk remarkably lucidly about this.'

'I'm not . . .'

'I had the impression, perhaps I'm wrong, that people in your state could barely summon up energy to creep out of bed.'

'Some days. That's right. But then, on others I can look for my touchpapers or touchstones, my stimulators.'

'So. I see. Well, round the course again.' Her choice of words confirmed to herself that she indulged, spoilt her companion. Gillian waited for no further order, turned on her heel, strode away.

'Keep up,' she called. 'This is good exercise.' The journey was quickly, fiercely over, and when they reached the car Gill panted, breathing shallowly, 'That was great. Thanks.'

'Not once more?' Liz, chancing it.

'Enough's enough. You don't understand what I'm up to, do you? Never mind. Let's get in and chase back home.'

'Seat belt,' Liz warned.

'I wouldn't mind dying some days. Not now. I've enjoyed this. It'll keep me going until Christmas.'

The rest of the journey was uneventful, with Gillian, the ideal passenger, silent in tricky periods, interestingly conversational along the flatness of roads. In the darkness outside her front gate Gill delivered a pretty speech, slightly long, then elegantly stepped out, waved and made off.

Before Christmas they met twice, once for shopping, once for a party at the house of the senior Paiges.

'Do you really want to go?' Liz asked David.

'Yes. They'll make a fuss of us. I've no irons in the fire there. I quite like Tony.'

'Isn't he a bit ineffective?' Liz enjoyed these dressing-room exchanges, when they could take their time, change their minds, peer into mirrors and slightly excited by the prospect of an outing ask questions, pass information, talk intimately.

'Oh, no. Don't think so. He likes to give that impression. And so does the old chap. But in fact he's considerably enlarged the garage business. I'd say he's a good head on him.' He'd changed his tune, or turned generous.

'You'd employ him?'

'As what?'

She laughed at her husband's caution; he'd answer only questions that were precise and within his strictly set bounds. He grinned because he knew why she was amused, and approved. No fools in this family.

At the house of the Philip Paiges, Gill cut a shining figure, but was verbally restrained, hardly drinking, helping to dispense hospitality. The old man cornered Elizabeth, congratulated her on success with his daughter-in-law.

'We're an old-fashioned family,' he said. 'We talk things over. Anthony has lunch with us at least twice a week, and Eileen goes to "Linacre" every Friday. So we know what you've been up to, and we know what you'll say: that you haven't done anything. We heard about your seaside jaunt. She'll talk now, will our Gill. To us, I mean. She'd say things to Anthony before, and he'd tell us, but now she comes across herself. That's good. She's improving.'

'You didn't like her.'

'Don't mean in that way. We didn't much, to tell you the truth. Hoity-toity Oxford miss. He met her there, you know. But he thinks something of her. Christ knows why, especially the ta-ta she's led him. But I think he's taming her.'

'David says he's good at business.'

'He is. I didn't think he would be. He went to Oxford University and all that. I suppose it taught him how to speak to people and which knife and fork to use. But he's learnt this business very, very fast. He's terrified me, I'll tell you. I've sat there peeing myself,' he peered for reaction, mischievously with his red-rimmed eyes, 'when I've realized what he's been up to, but he's pulled it off. He's building on solid foundations. You realize that.' They laughed; she liked ironical self-awareness. This porcine old man with his full whisky glass was worth her cultivation.

'Is Gill a help, do you think?'

'I don't think she's been so. No. She's had a tottering time, and I wouldn't bet she was out of the wood yet, but Eileen was only saying last night that she seems to have come to terms with her life. She'll always be a bird of paradise; dressed up in fine raiment. And she can carry it off, I don't deny. But she knows she's comfortably provided for, and will be more so. She's what? Thirty, thirty-one now? She's settling.'

'What about a family?'

'What about it? That's what I ask them. "There's time," they say. And look down their noses. And while we're on with it, what about an increase from you? What do you say to that?'

'Your vocabulary's Shakespearian.'

'And my aunt's moggy's name's Fanny.'

'We talk about it,' Liz said, smiling at the paunch, the upper lip stubbled with grey bristle, the spectacles snatched on and off, the red flesh of cheeks.

'We're all one-child families. We are. The Wincantons are. Your David's an only. Were you?'

'No. Two brothers and a sister. All older, and all abroad.'

'We lost two before we had Anthony. One stillborn, one miss. And no sooner was he born than I came out of the army. Rum bloody life. Not fertile, some of us. That's why it was daft, they say, to marry an heiress. She had so much because there weren't so many of them.'

Eileen Paige prised Liz away from her husband, adding her

splutter of thanks. She seemed ladylike, diffident, nicely spoken, unlike the old man who had barely mastered the aitch.

Eating and drinking was heavy and hearty; shouting no one frowned on. Childish games of musical chairs, vociferously encored, forfeits, postman's knock, hunt the thimble, were thumped through. Gill performed more readily than Elizabeth; holding hands with, bowing to her father-in-law's middle-aged and elderly friends; poised, she did not despise, though she discouraged familiarity. When the guests sank sweating to their seats they were issued with paper and pencils for 'Consequences'. David Watson met Gillian Paige (oooh-ooh) behind the cowshed (what bucolic childhood was restored in that phrase?). He said, 'I think I shall buy a new, red car' (moderate disappointment). She said, 'What have you done with my knickers?' (Sensation; the ladies as raucously amused as the men, guessing who was responsible. Gill unperturbed, smiled and folded her hands.) The consequence was he had to go to the General Hospital. (Ribald suggestions, forehead- and pate-wiping, tears dabbed dry, one more button undone, drinks gladly grabbed.) Liz felt herself distanced, approving of the noisy innocence, but finding herself incapable of joining with enjoyment. At the height of one romp, 'A-hunting we will go', David raised a white hand to her, a small, formal, diplomatic gesture and motion of confidence; the brief acknowledgement of her presence cheered.

'This is their idea of an orgy,' Anthony Paige said, coming up behind her during the collapse after the dance.

'They're enjoying themselves.'

'Do you think so? I guess most of 'em would as soon sit glooming with a glass in their fist. But all this energy expended is Dad's idea. I don't know whether he's getting his own back, or what.'

'Are they business associates?'

'Yes. And people from the village.' Tony named names,

concerns, fortunes, and once or twice histories. All were successful; a retired trade-union knight nodded his head nearer the bosom of a factory-owning tyrant; the relict of a millionaire scrap-dealer stroked or clutched the black cloth of a canon's sleeve.

They tried charades, crudely, but lacked the heart to do well. They wanted to hark back to the nursery and the Sunday school so that they flopped and bawled sweatingly through 'Oranges and Lemons' until Liz thought a dozen cardiac arrests were imminent. The average age must have been over fifty; one or two of the dancers topped seventy and yet enthusiasm boiled. Huge glass jugs of iced lemonade appeared, were emptied.

'Haven't tasted this stuff since I was a nipper.'

' 'Tin't bad, is it?'

Philip Paige beamed and mopped, initiated duels with balloons, but he'd worn his guests out so that they sprawled in easy chairs and watched the younger fry, Tony and Liz, Gillian and David, four more partners waltz, where the carpet had been rolled back, to the sedate Victor Sylvester.

'Your father's pleased with you,' Liz told Tony.

'He's pleased with himself, and that makes him generous.'

'Do you enjoy this?' Gill asked her partner.

'It's unusual. Never seen anything like it since I was a child.'

'That's good, isn't it?' They made a striking pair.

The hot sausage rolls appeared, but appetites were jaded now, digestion soured. Liz and David deserted the majority of comatose guests before midnight, drove home in blue moonlight, laughing and impressed.

On the next night, Christmas Eve, as they sat together filling Miranda's stocking, a performance both enjoyed because David visibly admired the abundant variety of small gifts his wife had assembled, she reported what old Paige had said about Gillian, asked if he thought it right.

'To some extent,' he said. 'She's had another short affair lately.'

'And it's over?'

'I think so. One can't be sure.'

'Does Tony . . . ?'

'No idea.'

'It's terrible.'

'I don't know. He may have made up his mind to connive at it. Perhaps it doesn't matter.'

'He's keen on her. He'll look after her, says so. I can't see him not minding her flying off with any man who attracts her attention.'

'Maybe you're right. I'm not claiming she's wildly promiscuous. I don't know.'

'Will they have children?' Liz asked.

'No idea. Probably not. Shouldn't think she's too keen. But she changes her mind.'

'So do we all.'

They could hear Miranda singing to herself in bed. She'd determined to retire early, but now, too excited to sleep, she carolled, violently rolling her head on the pillow. This year, for the first time, she had brought, made or procured their presents without help, and had told the headmaster of her school that she hoped they had Christmas in heaven because she didn't want her grandfather to miss it.

'What did Mr Owen say to that?' David asked.

'He didn't think they needed Christmas. They had received their reward. They didn't lack anything.'

'And what did Miss think?' David now.

'She argued that if you had everything you wanted it would be dull.'

'If they're all like her, Owen must have his work cut out.' David, pleased.

'He's chapel Welsh. He knows things.' Now she smiled. 'Philip Paige said it was time we had another child.' Her

185

husband merely put his hands together, looking up at her. Then both nodded, not meaning that this was agreed, but that a pleasant topic had been noted for future fare. Miranda appeared solemnly at the door, but not before her mother had hidden the stocking behind her.

'What are you doing?' the girl inquired.

'We might ask you the same question,' David said, giving his wife time to complete the camouflage.

'I thought I'd come down in case there was something interesting happening.'

'Mummy and I are talking,' David answering, taking Mirry on his knee, straightening and buttoning her dressing-gown.

'Boring, grown-up conversation,' the child announced.

'Why aren't you asleep?' The mother. 'It's well past your usual time and you've been up there nearly an hour and a half.'

'I think I'm too excited.'

'If you went off to sleep the morning would be here all the quicker.'

'I know. I said that to myself. But it made no difference.'

'What are we to do for you, then?' David.

'I would like a drink, please. No. Cold. Lemon barley. And a biscuit. It's Christmas Eve. I'll clean my teeth again. And perhaps if Daddy read me a story, I'd begin to feel tired.'

'Why should Christmas Eve make any difference?' David.

'Because it's itself. People have holidays; they don't have to go to work tomorrow. They sing carols in the streets. Some sang at Mr Owen's house. It was for charity, he said.' She achieved a fair caricature of his Celtic rotundity.

Elizabeth fetched the drink and a chocolate finger.

'Nothing sad,' the child warned her father.

'Or long,' Liz added. 'We were up late last night. We feel like sleep, if you don't.'

'I'll say "Good King Wencelas",' the father promised.

'You should sing that.'

'You should be thankful with what you get.' He threatened her with a jovial fist.

'For what we are about to receive, may the Lord make us truly thankful. Amen. And one boy said, a big boy called Bobby Marsland, he said, "Tuck in" instead of "Amen".'

'And what did Father Owen say to that?'

'He didn't hear it. Only me.' She grinned slyly, in no hurry with her biscuit. Father recited, the ladies hummed 'Good King Wenceslas'; it was repeated *con brio*. David insisted that the child contribute a solo. She clambered down from his knee, tidied her appearance, and staring straight ahead, fair hair glistening, began,

> 'To Mercy, Pity, Peace and Love
> All pray in their distress;
> And to these virtues of delight
> Return their thankfulness.'

The voice followed no infantile singsong; perhaps it was too well-ordered, its crescendos and diminuendos carefully organized; Mr Owen's conducting had supplied an ample variety of pace, volume and pitch, but it had not spoilt the clarity of the voice nor the quizzical look as if the young mind tried to chase and hold the meaning which skipped ahead of the spoken words. Elizabeth was suddenly overwhelmed; one minute she listened to a partypiece and the next she was brought face to face with the rawness of poetry.

> 'For Mercy has a human heart,
> Pity a human face,
> And Love, the human form divine
> And Peace, the human dress.'

They congratulated Miranda, who refused another chocolate finger, and marched sedately to bed hand in hand with her father.

'That recitation was good, wasn't it?' David asked, returning.

'Owen's a pious old humbug,' she told him, 'but he makes me feel there's somebody left in the world who's bothering whether or not culture continues. I wouldn't leave the total choice to him, but . . .'

'Who wrote it?'

'Blake. *Songs of Innocence.*'

'I seem to remember some lad saying it on the Sunday school anniversary in Sheffield.'

He'd no idea, she realized, this Crane Street product, that this was anything but a bit of religious rhyming, nor that it had moved her so radically. She'd no power of explanation; she knew what he did not. The realization warmed her towards him so that she took his hand and kissed him.

He returned the kiss with a surprised passion.

'Just like Christmas,' he said, when they broke away.

Elizabeth finished filling the stocking before she went upstairs. Miranda lay asleep in a tousled bed, flushed but smiling. David tiptoed in to watch the straightening clothes; both bent to kiss the unmarked hair line.

'Do you ever get as excited as that?' Liz asked her husband, downstairs.

'I don't suppose so.'

'You're not the excitable sort,' she said drily.

'I look for snags. Yes.'

'Do you ever think your companies will go out of business?'

'You keep asking me that, Liz. No, I don't. We're big. We're solid and forward looking.'

She bent over the book she had not yet opened, looked at its fire-orange dust cover, stroked it, as if there was comfort to be found.

'Our profits are larger this year, by a long way, even in areas where rivals haven't done so well.'

'European rivals? German?'

'Yes. And don't forget we have factories there, and in the Low Countries.' He spoke very quietly, and the last words sounded dull, without rhetorical or historical flourish. 'You're not bored here? At home all day?'

'Sometimes. But it's my own fault. I'll try better next term.' She smiled. 'You shook me, too hard. I can't trust anything. I'm beginning to settle, but if I went to the doctor I'd expect him to find cancer. I don't want to keep on about it. I can't help it.'

In the course of the few sentences she found herself switched from domestic contentment to anxiety, to a bestial place where she'd leap up and fling her book into a greasy pit, at invisible writhing fears. That the trauma lay so near the surface shocked her, that its effect thrashed so violently shamed. Her breath seemed held, her rib-cage set in concrete pain. She had no idea whether or not she was crying.

'Are you all right?'

David stood over her, but she could not answer. Her totality of attention seemed bunched into a ball thrust down her throat into her chest, there to rankle, or suffocate. He touched her head and she did not feel it. She saw without observing.

'Elizabeth.' He repeated the name, and again, stroking her.

She heard the name. 'Elizabeth'. Scales fell. She breathed. Her body relaxed so that she smiled, snatched at his hand, kissed it.

'You went white as a sheet.'

She let go of his fingers.

'We're friends,' she said.

'Friends?' The word puzzled him. She thought he'd step away, but swaying, he held his ground. 'That's something.' He'd risk no more, not a joke, not a clown's smile, a me-Tarzan, you-Jane. They were two persons on a rich stage, but viewed now in the hung moment when the curtain rises and the audience only sees, knows nothing, can draw conclusions from clothes or face or posture or furniture but does not know. That husband and wife faced such frozen time, but without the anticipation of pleasure, silenced Liz for she realized that it described her, her alone. What he felt, thought, she did not know.

He touched her head, but lightly, not moving his hand. The cuff of his other sleeve dangled over purposeless fingers.

Now she must stand up, not for herself, for him.

She rose and, loudly, blatantly, plangently spouted.

> 'So we'll go not more a-roving
> By the light of the moon.'

He frowned, not with either distaste or puzzlement, but as if the skin of his face acted for him. He wanted to understand, to snatch communion with her if it were possible.

After some silent, not uncomfortable minutes, Elizabeth began to speak again.

'Those verses Mirry said were perfect. I like to step just inside her school sometimes, old Owen's kingdom. I go early, now and then, just to hang around. That's what the world ought to be like, all ordered, and sitting straight, and saying things and putting the bags and boxes away.'

'Aren't there any wrongdoers?' he asked, glad to join in.

'I hear some getting ticked off. And there is punishment. But it seems to work so that the headmaster can give an order and they all learn marvellous lines of poetry. And some will remember them until they're old men and women.'

'That's good,' he said.

'It's beginning to mend between me and you,' she answered. 'I couldn't believe it. The shock was so violent. I thought I'd never be able to trust anyone again.' He stretched a hand, towards which she nodded and smiled. 'Perhaps we're healed. I can't forget it.'

'Taff Owen has told us to be good,' David said.

'And we are.'

It seemed right; it needed some old-fashioned word to describe it: benison, some chapel concept, atonement, covenant. It was quietly magnificent, like Blake, writing the truth in cold water. Just over a week later, on the first of January, she and Gillian Paige walked upstairs in the early hours from the laughter, the arrival after midnight of the dark stranger, the good wishes, to stand together in a bedroom looking out over cold roofs, black trees, a thickness of cloud. Bells clashed, though downstairs they were inaudible, from a church just below them, on the main city road, fearsome almost, powerfully, breathlessly metallic.

'Say something now,' Gill said.

> ' "Ring out, wild bells to the wild sky,
>   The flying cloud, the frosty light:
>   The year is dying in the night:
>   Ring out, wild bells, and let him die." '

'No flying clouds here,' Gill complained, craning. 'So much for milord Tennyson.'

'It's beginning to snow.'

'So it is.'

The flakes dropped, skimmed, staggered down. By the next morning the slight ground-cover had melted, but for the moment snow fell into the cold of a new year.

'I hate bloody Tennyson,' Gill said. ' "Larger heart and kindlier hand." I could puke.'

'He starts with poetry, and then says the right thing.'

Elizabeth took her hand, wrapped fingers in fingers, and stood watching the tumble of snowflakes. A door opened downstairs and muzak burst, blaring over the voices. They could hear old man Paige in the hall, bawling encouragement to some backslider from drunken enjoyment.

'Ring out, wild bells,' Liz laughed.

A benison fell, would fall again.